Caterpillar Jones and the Adventures of Nut E. Squirrel

J.J. Brothers

FOUNDATION PUBLISHING

FOUNDATION PUBLISHING
P.O. BOX 296
GREEN, OHIO 44232

Visit J.J. Brothers online at:
www.caterpillarjones.com

ISBN: 0-9718774-0-8

First trade paperback printing
April 2002.

10 9 8 7 6 5 4 3 2

Printed in the U.S.A.

10/24/11

This book is dedicated to all the children,
like us, who have spent their lives
struggling with weight issues.

To Sydney

Enjoy   Thankyou
             For
             Saving
             us!

The

Adventure!!

J.J. Birtn

Acknowledgments

We would first like to thank Amy Jo Sutterluety, Donna Fleck, and Nancy Ulrich for providing us with the information that made this book possible. Your knowledge of health, and your expertise was invaluable. Thank you for all the work you do on a daily basis helping our children to live healthier lives.

Again, we want to thank Peter Orullian for making our words flow more smoothly, and Michelle Fryer for being the best publicist in the world.

Ben Brenneman, for his fabulous illustrations that have made this book come to life.

And lastly, we would like to thank our friends and family whose undying support and guidance has made our dream a reality.

Contents

A New Adventure

Sammy and I had some cloud climbing to do that morning, and I was so excited that I could hardly contain myself. My heart pounded as I quickly flew behind Sammy desperately trying to keep up with him. Sammy was my best friend, and the bravest adventurer I have ever known. Being a caterpillar had been a lot of fun, but now that we were butterflies, our lives were absolutely amazing. Each day was a new adventure, and today's adventure was going to take us higher and further than any other butterfly had gone before, but first we needed permission from our wives.

My wife, Cat, and Sammy's wife, Sandy, were waiting for us at the Mulberry Bush. The Mulberry Bush is where all the butterflies lay their eggs for the winter, and it is nestled on the edge of a large, green valley known as Mulberry Meadow. This is where we had all grown up as caterpillars. As we made our way towards the bush, I couldn't help but think about all the adventures that Sammy and I had experienced the previous summer. We had cloud climbed with Clarence and George several times. We'd surfed on leaves, discovered new and tasty flowers no one had ever seen before, and we even found time to Mirror Fly with our wives.

It had been a great summer, but it was now coming to an end. It would soon be time for us to migrate south to a place called Butterfly Island. Most of the other flying animals had already left for the winter, and the rest were busy storing food for the long cold months ahead. The normal activity of the meadow was now replaced by a quiet peacefulness.

When we finally arrived at the Mulberry Bush, we quickly realized that Cat and Sandy were a little upset.

"Where have you two been?" Cat asked angrily. "I can't believe that you guys were out goofing off on the day that Sandy and I are supposed to leave for Butterfly Island."

I looked over at Sammy, but he just stared at the ground.

"Yeah," Sandy added. "Once, we are gone, you two are going to have a full month to do whatever you want. The least you two could have done was spend some quality time with us before we leave."

I felt kind of bad; Sandy was right. Sammy and I were

2

so caught up in the climb we were about to make that we didn't take time to realize the sacrifices that the girls were making for all of us. They had agreed to fly down early to Butterfly Island in order to set up our winter homes. Sammy and I were going to stay behind for a few weeks to watch the meadow and make sure everything was going smoothly. At least, that's what we told our wives. The real reason we were staying was to get in some quality adventuring. We didn't know it at the time, but that decision would change our lives forever.

"Don't you understand, Jones?" Cat said. "All the other butterflies have already left. If we don't leave now, we are not going to get a good spot."

"I can't believe you guys," Sandy added, shaking her head back and forth. "Between Clarence and George having to be the *first* ones to migrate to Butterfly Island, and you and Sammy having to be the *last* ones, I don't know who is more ridiculous."

Just then, Sammy looked up at Sandy. "Clarence and George?" he said with a proud look on his face. "It's nothing to be the first ones to migrate, but it takes *true* adventurers to be the last ones. Obviously, we are the ones who are more ridiculous."

When the girls heard this, they looked at each other and began laughing. Their anger quickly faded, as they came over and hugged us both. *I can't believe it*, I thought to myself. *Sammy has done it again*. His humor had got us out of another sticky situation.

"I love you Cat," I said. "And I want you girls to be

careful. It's a long flight, and there are a lot of dangers between here and Butterfly Island. It's like Mayor Nut E. Squirrel always says 'It's a lot safer to be careful than to be carefree.'"

Sammy rolled his eyes and sighed. "Ahh man, here he goes with the Nut E. Squirrel stories again."

I looked at Sammy confused. "What are you talking about?" I asked.

"C.J., you are constantly quoting the Mayor," Sammy replied, rolling his eyes. "And you have never even met him."

"Sammy, from what I have heard, Nut E. Squirrel is one of the greatest animals that has ever lived. And I just think he is someone to be looked up to. He has done a lot of great things."

Suddenly, I thought of a good story to explain what I meant. "Did I ever tell you guys the story of how Nut E. Squirrel got his name." No one answered. "Well, as you know, his real name is Nuthaniel Eaton Squirrel. But when he was a kid, he ate so many nuts, that one day his mother just looked at him and said—"

Sammy, Sandy, and Cat all jumped in at once and shouted: "That's one nut eating squirrel!"

I felt a little embarrassed as they all began laughing. Obviously, I had told the story too many times before. Cat was still smiling as she flew over, hugged me tight, and said, "And later, his name was shortened to Nut E. Squirrel. We know, Jones. You must have told that story a hundred times."

"A hundred and one," I joked, acting like I wasn't embarrassed.

"Oh Jones, I'm going to miss you so much"

"Don't worry, Cat," I said. "Sammy and I are just going to hang around here for a few weeks, and we will be down to Butterfly Island before you know it."

"Okay," Cat said reluctantly. "Go ahead and have your fun, but just remember that next year things are going to be a lot different."

I smiled as I realized what she meant. "That reminds me, Cat. Where are they?"

"Right down there," Cat said, pointing at a lower branch of the Mulberry Bush.

We all flew down towards the bottom of the bush, and when we did, we saw them. There were two brand new egg sacks attached to the bottom limb. One belonged to Cat and I, and the other to Sammy and Sandy. Sammy and I had insisted that the girls lay their eggs on the lowest branch of the bush down below all the other butterfly eggs. We decided this would give our children a head start, and would allow them to be the first caterpillars to reach the ground and begin their many adventures. When I looked at the egg that held my future child, I couldn't help but feel proud. *Cat is right*, I thought to myself. *Things were going to be different next year*. I was going to be a father, and I could hardly wait.

When we said goodbye to our wives, everybody cried. I was really looking forward to the month of excitement that Sammy and I had planned, but I was going to miss

Cat. I was now more in love with her than ever before. And as I watched her fly over and kiss the tiny egg sack goodbye, I realized what a wonderful mother she was going to make.

Cat flew over to me one last time and said, "I love you, Jones. Please, be careful."

"You be careful, too, Cat," I replied. "And don't worry. Sammy and I will look after the eggs while you are gone. They will be fine. I promise."

Cat smiled as she and Sandy said their final "goodbyes" and reluctantly began to make their way south.

As they disappeared over the horizon, Sammy looked at me and said, "Well, it's official, C.J. We are now the only butterflies left in Mulberry Meadow, and we have a full month before we have to leave. There is nothing for us to do but Cloud Climb, and today's Cloud Climb is going to be a record breaker. We are going to climb to the highest cloud in the history of the meadow."

As Sammy continued talking about our climb, I found myself staring at the little green and yellow egg sack that hung from the bottom branch of the Mulberry Bush. Ignoring Sammy, I flew over and hovered beside the egg.

"Don't worry, my little adventurer," I whispered. "You're going to be alone for now, while your mother and I are down at Butterfly Island. But when spring comes, you'll hatch into a brave little caterpillar. You are going to have a lot of fun that summer, and when you are ready, you are going to turn into a beautiful butterfly. That's when we will meet, and when we do, we are going to have a lot of fun together. Oh, I can't wait to teach you about Cloud Climbing, and all the other adventures that lie ahead of you, and I am looking forward to the day where we can go Cloud Climbing together."

After I finished talking to my egg, Sammy and I began that long familiar climb into the sky. As we lifted off the ground, and began heading towards the clouds, the view was breathtaking. I could see for miles in all directions. You see Mulberry Meadow is only a part of the neighborhood in which we live. This area is called Section 7, and Mulberry Meadow only makes up half of it. Section 7 is divided by a large river. On the other side of the river is a big group of trees known as Tree Ville. From our height, Section 7 was beginning to look like a small dot beneath us. There are several different sections up and down the river, and from up here, I could see them all.

As we continued climbing, I began to get excited thinking about all the fun that Sammy and I were going to have over the next few weeks. Sammy had it all planned out. We were going to spend most of our time perfecting our Cloud Climbing skills. Any spare time we might have would be spent searching for new adventures. The other butterflies didn't know what they were missing. They were so busy racing down to Butterfly Island that they didn't realize they were missing one of the best times to be in the meadow. The weather was still warm, but as we climbed higher and higher in the sky, the air started to get a little chilly. Clarence and George had warned us that Cloud Climbing so late in the year could be very dangerous, because at this height, the water on our wings could freeze. But Sammy said that they were just worried we might break their record, and that we shouldn't pay any attention to them. The wind was blowing us around harder than before. And the higher we went, the colder it became. I began to get nervous, and it reminded me of how scared I was the first time I went Cloud Climbing.

"It's awfully cold up here, Sammy," I said. "Maybe Clarence and George were right. Maybe we should just forget about this climb, and start heading south right now."

Sammy flew up next to me and said, "Don't worry, C.J., we have plenty of time. As long as we start migrating before it snows, we can make it to Butterfly Island just fine. We could stay at least another month before we would have trouble leaving. All the other butterflies were just in a hurry."

After Sammy said this, he quickly flew up towards the clouds and said

"Come on, C.J.! If you keep climbing that slowly, your wings will freeze for sure. Remember, speed is a Cloud Climbers friend."

Then, Sammy pulled away and yelled back, "I will see you in the light my friend."

My heart raced as I watched Sammy disappear into the clouds.

I quickly followed after him, plunging into the dense, moist air of the cloud. It immediately surrounded my entire body like an egg sack. Trying to make my way to the top, I began beating my wings extra hard to keep the moisture off of them like we had done so many times before. I looked forward to the moment when I would finally break through the top of the cloud and meet the sun's brilliant, warm glow signifying another successful Cloud Climb.

But today something was different. The cloud was thicker, and colder than usual. Soon, the water on my wings began to freeze. This had never happened before, and no matter how hard I flapped my wings, I couldn't get the ice off of them. My wings grew heavy, and I could hardly move them. I knew I wasn't going to make it to the top. So, I spun around, and dove towards the bottom of the cloud.

I flew as fast as I could, but by the time I broke free from the thick mist, my wings were frozen solid, and I could not move them at all. My heart pounded as I plummeted towards the ground. I quickly rolled over on my back trying to slow myself down. As I wheeled around, I saw Sammy burst from the side of the cloud. He was in trouble too. He was sputtering out of control, and could barely move his wings. Then he did something truly amazing, even for Sammy. He purposely threw himself into a tight, spinning nosedive. This is something butterflies don't do, because it is nearly impossible to pull out of one, but Sammy had no choice. He was desperate. I wasn't sure what he was trying to do, until he snapped open his wings and the ice shattered off of them flying everywhere. Free of the ice, Sammy was able to fly again.

With great effort, he was able to pull out of the dive, and then he began heading towards me.

Knowing that he would not be able to reach me in time, he started screaming, "C.J., pull up! Pull up! You're going to hit the ground!"

"But Sammy, I can't move my wings," I screamed as I rolled over onto my stomach.

I was trying not to panic, but I was running out of time.

I was quickly falling down towards the Tree of Life, when I saw something. I couldn't believe my luck. There was a giant net made of silk Traveling Thread attached to one of the limbs. "I can make it," I thought to myself. "I can land in the net, and stop my fall." The ice was starting to break away from my wings, and I was now able to move them just enough to glide towards the net. I lined myself up perfectly, but I was coming in a little too fast. I closed my eyes and braced for impact.

Pain shot through my entire body as I hit the net at top speed. The Traveling Thread stretched but it didn't break. It sprang back and forth, shaking every limb of the tree. When the net finally came to a stop, my heart was still racing, but at least I was safe. I was starting to calm down, when Sammy flew in and landed on a limb next to me.

"C.J., that was amazing. I can't believe this net is here. You are the luckiest butterfly I have ever seen."

Exhausted, I looked at Sammy and said, "Sammy, can we go to Butterfly Island now?"

Sammy just laughed and reached down to help me up out of the net. But as he tried to pull me out, I realized that this Traveling Thread was different from the thread we'd used as caterpillars. It was very sticky, and I was finding it nearly impossible to break free from it. Sammy grabbed my arm, and flew up into the air. He pulled as hard as he could, but when he did, the net stretched towards him, but I was still stuck to it. Sammy kept pulling until the net wouldn't stretch any further. When Sammy got tired, the net sprang backwards, pulling Sammy in with me. We were both trapped and covered in the sticky silk thread. When we realized we were both stuck, we started laughing hysterically.

"You know, C.J.," Sammy said, "Maybe this final Cloud Climb wasn't such a good idea. After all, part of being an adventurer is being smart enough to know when something is *too* dangerous to do."

Just then, I felt the net move underneath me. "Sammy, was that you? Were you moving?"

Sammy looked at me concerned and said

"No, it wasn't me."

We slowly turned our heads towards the top of the net from where the movement was coming from and I saw the biggest spider I had ever seen in my life. It was three times bigger than Sammy and I put together. Thick, bristly hair covered all eight of its long, black legs. It stepped very carefully along the net, as if it were dancing towards us. With each step, the net vibrated, sending chills down my spine. As the spider came closer, we could see his razor sharp teeth grinding together. We instantly began thrashing against the sticky prison, trying to free ourselves from the net. But the more we struggled, the more entangled we became. It seemed hopeless.

Sammy turned and looked at me. "C.J., this isn't good," he said.

As I watched Sammy desperately trying to think of a way out, I couldn't help but think that this was all my fault. *Why didn't we just leave with the rest of the butterflies?* I thought to myself. Terror struck me, and I began to shake uncontrollably as the spider moved closer and closer to us.

Then, all of the sudden, he stopped. The immense spider whirled around, turning its back on us. When I looked up, I saw what the spider was staring at. From out of the shadows, a brown squirrel emerged. Carrying a large, wooden staff, the squirrel strode confidently, his muscles rippling. I had never seen this squirrel in the meadow before, but the spider seemed to know who he was. They stood there staring at each other for several minutes without moving a muscle. Then the spider spoke.

"What are you doing here Champion?" he glared

The squirrel looked into the spider's eyes and slowly shook his head back and forth. "Not today, Shadow." he said. "You can't have these two."

Suddenly, Shadow reared back and started swinging his legs at the squirrel he called Champion. The squirrel quickly raised his staff, blocking each leg one after another. No matter how hard the spider tried, he could not hit the squirrel. Sammy and I couldn't believe Champion's skill. He moved effortlessly, swinging his staff like it was a part of him. The two warriors remained locked in a fierce battle for a very long time. At one point, Shadow swept the squirrel's legs and knocked him onto his back. The spider opened his mouth, and lunged forward, but before he could bite him, Champion raised his staff, shoving it into Shadow's opened mouth. The spider bit down on the weapon instinctively. Champion then spun the staff and flipped Shadow over. Using his tail as a springboard, the squirrel flipped himself back up onto his feet. I had never seen anyone move like Champion; his reflexes were unmatched, and yet at the same time, he was incredibly graceful.

Shadow quickly bounced back to his feet, and charged Champion. The squirrel swung his staff down and hit the spider on the head, stopping him cold. Using his staff, Champion pole-vaulted over the spider, and prepared to strike him again on the back. Before the squirrel could do it, Shadow shot a line of Traveling Thread into Champion's eyes, blinding him just like I had done to E. Phil Snake so long ago. The spider then spun around as the squirrel desperately tried to remove the thread. But the sticky webbing would not budge.

Then Champion did something truly amazing. He stopped struggling. He held his staff out in front of him, and stood there in silence as though he was listening to the spider's movements. Shadow slowly circled around him, and though the spider hardly made a sound,

Champion seemed to know where he was at all times. Again, Shadow charged, swinging his legs around wildly. Although the squirrel couldn't see, he blocked each and every leg just as he had done before.

But Shadow's constant blows proved to be too much. Champion's grip loosened, and the staff flew out of his hands. Standing there defenseless, he took a step back, and stood there again in silence. Our hopes for survival disappeared when Champion turned around and began running away towards the trunk of the tree. Not wanting to let his opponent off that easy, Shadow chased after him. When Champion reached the trunk of the tree, the spider was right behind him. I thought Champion would have to stop, but he didn't. Instead, the squirrel ran up the tree trunk, did a full back flip and landed right on top of the confused spider. Champion's weight buckled Shadow's legs and flattened him. The spider lay dazed. The squirrel then jumped off Shadow's back, grabbed one of the spider's back legs, and began spinning him around in a circle. When he had picked up enough speed, he let go, and Shadow went flying off of the tree.

Sammy and I just sat there not knowing what to say as the squirrel slowly wiped the traveling thread from his eyes, picked up his staff, and walked towards us. Without saying a word, he cut through the net with his staff, and we were free. We jumped up onto our feet, and began pulling the sticky traveling thread from our wings. We wanted to thank the squirrel for what he had done for us, but just as fast as he had appeared, he was gone. It seemed as though he vanished into thin air.

"Wow, that was unbelievable! Who was that squirrel?" I asked.

"I don't know," Sammy replied. "But I need to get myself one of those staffs."

We both laughed, and finished removing the Traveling Thread from our bodies. We were grateful to be alive, but a gust of cold wind quickly reminded us that there would be no more Cloud Climbing for the season.

"Well so much for Cloud Climbing, C.J.," Sammy said, disappointed.

"What are we going to do now?" I asked. "We have three weeks left, and nothing to do."

We both sat there in silence desperately trying to think of something else to do. After awhile, I finally said, "Sammy this is going to be boring. Maybe we should just go catch up with the girls and head down to Butterfly Island now."

"No, C.J.," Sammy argued. "We can't give up that easy. We just need to find a new adventure. That's all. Something that we have never done before."

"Like what, Sammy? I can't think of anything."

Just then, we heard a familiar voice coming from down below. It was our old scatterbrained friend Peety the Chipmunk. He was overly excited as he came scurrying up to us.

"I just saw a flying spider," he said. "I didn't know spiders could fly. Did you know they could fly? I didn't know they could fly. I wish *I* could fly. Don't you wish *you* could fly? Oh wait. Crimeney sakes, what am I saying, you *CAN* fly. I remember when you *couldn't* fly. And now you *can* fly. I even remember when that *spider* couldn't fly. And now he *can* fly. How come *I'm* the only one who *can't* fly? I really do need to learn how to fly."

As Peety rambled on, Sammy interrupted him. "Hey, Peety, you will never believe what happened to us. We got caught in this spider's net...and this really unbelievable squirrel saved us. He started flipping and spinning, and swinging this staff around. He was amazing!"

"Oh, you mean Champion," Peety said,

"Yeah, Champion," Sammy echoed. "I think that was his name."

Sammy and I listened carefully as Peety went on to explain that Champion Squirrel was a natural warrior who was personally trained by The Great Owl of Light himself. Peety said the warrior squirrel lived at the top of The Tree of Life. We wanted to go up to thank him, but Peety said that Champion was very mysterious and that he didn't like visitors, so we decided not to go.

As he spoke, Peety seemed more excited than usual. When we asked him why, he explained that The Great Owl of Light had left the meadow to take care of some important business, and had left Peety in charge.

"Yep, he left me in charge of the entire meadow," Peety said proudly. The energetic Peety smiled and spoke quickly, becoming more excited all the time. "I thought he was going to pick Champion; but he didn't, he chose me. Well he didn't actually say me. But I could tell by the way he was acting when he left that he expected me to stand in for him while he was gone. It must be due to my military background. I'm pretty sure I served in some sort of army once. Otherwise, why would he leave me in charge of the meadow? It's a very important job to be in charge of the meadow! Anyway, I'm in charge! I am the big kahuna! I'm the head honcho! The big cheese! I am Mother Nature's Right Hand Munk . . . I'm the—"

"Excuse me Peety," Sammy interrupted. "We really have to get going. C.J. and I are in search of a new adventure."

Peety looked shocked. "Crimeney sakes, you can't leave now."

"Why not?" I asked.

"You'll miss the emergency Section 7 meeting over in Tree Ville," Peety said. "You have to go. Somebody has got to represent the butterflies. Aren't you the only ones left? I can't represent the butterflies; I have to represent The Owl. You gotta remember, I'm the acting Owl. I'm in charge! I'm the big kahuna! I'm the head honcho! I'm the . . ."

As Peety rambled on, Sammy looked at me and asked, "So what do you say, C.J.? Do you want to go to this meeting?"

I thought for a moment. "I don't know . . . It sounds kind of boring."

Sammy just shrugged his shoulders. "Well, you never

know, C.J. This may be just the adventure we are looking for."

Since we had nothing better to do at the moment, I agreed to go, but as we made our way down the tree, I quickly began to regret my decision. I had been to these meetings before, and they were all the same—boring! The Deputy Mayor, Kip the chipmunk—who was also Peety's cousin—would get up in front of the crowd and talk for hours about things that had nothing to do with the butterflies. Usually these meetings were a complete waste of our time, and I wasn't looking forward to it at all.

"So, Peety, what incredibly exciting news is your cousin Kip going to talk about today?" I asked sarcastically.

"Oh, today is much different," Peety said with excitement. "No, not the same at all. This meeting is going to be much different much different indeed. Kip's not speaking. Oh no, no. Today we are actually going to hear from the Mayor himself. Yep, today is going to be much different."

I couldn't believe what I was hearing. I stopped dead in my tracks and looked at Peety in shock. "Peety, " I asked. "Do you mean to tell me that Mayor Nuthaniel Eaton Squirrel is actually going to be at the meeting today? Ahh man, this changes everything!"

Sammy just smiled and said, "So C.J, does this mean you want to go to the meeting?"

"Are you kidding me? I wouldn't miss it for the world. It's not every day that you get the chance to meet your personal hero."

A NEW ADVENTURE

I was now more excited than ever. *This is going to be great!* I thought to myself. Ever since I had become a butterfly, I had heard about all the wonderful things the Mayor had done not only for us in Section 7, but for all the other sections as well. They say that he had single handedly saved the river once, and that every one of us owed our lives to this amazing squirrel. I couldn't believe my luck. Today, I was actually going to get a chance to meet him.

I was extremely excited as we made our way out of Mulberry Meadow, over a small hill, and down towards the river bank. Normally, we would have just flown across the river but since we were with Peety, we had to stop and wait at Turtle Crossing. Turtle Crossing was a ferry service run by two flat-backed turtles. These turtles carried smaller animals across the river on their backs. They swam back and forth from bank to bank, staying in their own lanes, transporting animals that couldn't fly. Usually this service ran very smoothly, but because of the meeting, the traffic at Turtle Crossing was extremely high, and the turtles were behind schedule. Peety had to wait at Turtle Crossing for quite a while, and he became very impatient. So when Peety saw the turtle coming to pick him up, he said, "It's about time! I got an important meeting to go to! And I'm an important chipmunk. I can't stand around here all day waiting on turtles."

The turtle rolled his eyes. "Whatever, Peety. Just so you know, because of all this traffic the turtle tolls are higher today. It will be two red berries and one blue."

This made Peety very angry.

"This is ridiculous! You turtles are out of control! The meadow has no room for this selfish behavior. Two reds and a blue, that is outrageous!" Peety continued to protest as he handed the turtle the berries. "This is preposterous! The Owl should do something about this. Crimminey sakes, The Owl is not here. He put me in charge. I should do something about this. But I don't have time right now. I've got an important meeting to get to."

Peety got on the turtle's back and began the trip across the river. Sammy and I flew along beside him. As we slowly made our way across the river, Peety continued to complain. It was very obvious that he was taking his new role very seriously, even though no body else was.

"What in the world is taking so long?" Peety groaned. "I can not be late for this meeting. I am a high-ranking military official. I have to get there as soon as possible!"

The turtle told Peety that it wasn't his fault. He said that the river had swelled, and that he was having to swim further. Peety ignored the turtle, and kept rambling on about how lazy the turtles had become. The turtle didn't pay much attention to Peety. He just kept swimming. As the two turtles passed each other in the middle of the river, the one Peety was riding on looked at the other and said, "How's it going, Martin?"

"Not bad, Lewis," the other turtle said.

Peety quickly interrupted. "What is going on here? We don't have time for socializing."

Lewis shook his head in frustration. "Peety, if you

don't stop complaining, you're going to end up swimming the rest of the way."

Peety's jaw dropped. "That statement is bordering on insubordination, mister. You obviously have an attitude problem. And let me tell you, there is no 'I' in the word attitude . . . Crimmeny sakes, there is an "I" in the word attitude. What was I thinking?"

"I'm warning you, Peety." Lewis said trying to remain calm.

"This is ridiculous," Peety snapped back. "The Owl could have hired ducks instead. After all The Owl has done for you, you should be a little more appreciative. He's bent over backwards for you turtles. And since I'm the acting Owl, you should do what ever I say; you should even be willing to do back flips if I ask you."

At that point, Lewis stopped swimming, looked back at Peety and said, "Peety what are you *rambling* about."

Peety was now so angry that he could barely speak. "I . . . I . . . want you to do back flips," Peety demanded.

"Okay, fine. You want me to do a back flip," Lewis quickly replied. "I'll give you a back flip."

Suddenly, Lewis kicked his back legs up into the air and flipped Peety head over heals into the water. Sammy and I couldn't help but laugh as Peety came up out of the water looking like a wet ball of fur. His arms were waving wildly in the air, and he was spitting water everywhere. In a complete panic, Peety furiously dog paddled his way to the shore. When he got there, he flopped on his back and began desperately gasping for air. When Lewis arrived at the shore, he looked down at Peety smiling. "How did you like that back flip?" he asked sarcastically.

Still trying to catch his breath, Peety gasped, "That was no back flip. That was insubordination."

Peety was still rambling as Sammy and I flew down and lifted him back up onto his feet.

"That's it! I am never going to take Turtle Crossing again. No matter how long it takes, I will find another way to get across. I am the acting Owl. I need to think more like him. What would he do? He would fly across! Crimmeny sakes, that's it! I will build a flying machine, and fly across! Yeah that's it, a flying machine. That way I can be exactly like The Owl and fly over my domain."

Peety became so involved in his new idea that he completely forgot about Sammy and I and walked off in the opposite direction.

"Peety where are you going?" Sammy yelled. "What about the meeting?"

Peety just threw up his hands and said, "I don't have time for that silly meeting anymore. I have more important things to attend to. I need to gather some supplies."

Peety continued rambling as he walked off down river. Sammy and I just stood there looking at each other for a moment, not quite knowing what to do next. But when we saw a large group of animals headed towards a clearing in the trees, we decided to follow them. At the time, we could have never guessed just how important it would be for us to attend this particular town meeting, but we were about to find out.

Meeting the Mayor

Sammy and I quickly made our way into Tree
Ville, which was a dense group of trees that
lined the river. It was usually a very crowded place
because so many animals made their home here, but it
seemed quiet now. I guess everyone was at the meeting.
Tree Ville was an exciting place where dreams came true,
and important decisions were made. This was my kind of
town, but Sammy preferred the peacefulness of Mulberry
Meadow. When we arrived at the meeting we were amazed
to see how many animals were there. Obviously, we
weren't the only ones who were excited to hear the Mayor
speak. The meeting was being held in a clearing in the
woods. At one end of the clearing stood a tree-stump
podium and just in front of the podium the other animals

gathered, anticipating the arrival of Mayor Nut E. Squirrel. You could almost feel the excitement in the air. Nobody seemed to know what the meeting was about, but if Nut E. planned to speak, it must be pretty big,

Weaving in and out of the crowd was a short, wide-eyed, fuzzy, brown and white chipmunk. It was Kip, the Deputy Mayor. He flipped through the pages of his leaf notebook as he ran around frantically trying to get everything ready for the meeting. Kip liked everything to be perfect. As Sammy and I took our places in the crowd, the Deputy Mayor came running up to us.

Gasping for breath, he spoke quickly, "Hey guys, I'm surprised to see you two are still here. I thought all the butterflies had already left."

"Most have," Sammy said. "We are the last ones."

"Well, I'm glad you could make it. Hey…listen…I have to apologize for the Mayor. He's been so busy that he hasn't had a chance to get over to Mulberry Meadow in a while. But that is all going to change soon."

I couldn't contain my excitement any longer. "Hey Kip, Peety said the Mayor was going to speak today, is that true?"

Kip smiled from ear to ear. "Yes it is. And after today, things are going to be a lot different around here."

"Why, what's going on?" Sammy asked, excited.

Kip just slowly shook his head. "Oh, I can't spoil the surprise. But let me tell you, it's big." Kip's eyes widened as he looked around at the overwhelming number of animals that continued to fill the small clearing.

"Wow!" Kip exclaimed. "There are an awful lot of animals here today." Then he thought for a moment and said, "You know, it's funny. We never get this kind of turn out when I speak."

Sammy and I just looked at each other and said nothing. Kip may not have been much of a speaker, but he *was* a good friend. He was a very kindhearted chipmunk and we liked him a great deal. Kip not only made us feel welcome, but he took time out of his busy schedule to introduce us to some of the animals that we didn't know.

Among these animals, we met Edna and Abner mouse. When we met them it didn't take us long to figure out that Edna was a very dominating mouse, who nagged her husband Abner all the time. She was very opinionated and she wasn't afraid to speak her mind. In fact when we met up with her she was complaining to Kip about how wet the ground was.

"I don't remember it raining," she complained. "Kip, why would you call a meeting with this much water on the ground? Do you expect us to tromp around in the mud all day?"

Kip apologized, but Edna brushed him off and walked away in a huff.

At that point, we heard a voice yelling "Peanuts . . . Sun roasted peanuts, here . . . a meeting is not a meeting unless you are eating . . . Peanuts . . . Sun roasted peanuts."

"Who's that?" Sammy asked

"Oh that's just Telly Vision" Kip said.

Kip explained that Telly was a ferret that sold food to

the citizens of Tree Ville. He was a very animated and persuasive sales animal. So when he came up to us and offered Sammy a nectar-filled flower, he couldn't resist.

"Hello, gentlemen, my name is Telly Vision, but you can call me TV. Now I didn't expect butterflies to still be here this time of year, but I do happen to have a couple nice, juicy roses just for you guys. They are bursting full of fresh, delicious, mouth-watering nectar. So step on up and have yourself a little power shower from the flower."

Sammy bought two roses and tucked them away for later.

Just then, someone tapped me on the shoulder. I turned to see Tree Ville's doctor, Rosie O'Rabbit. Black and white fur covered the older but healthy-looking rabbit. She was very straightforward, and talked with a slight Irish accent. During our many adventures the previous summer, Sammy and I had come to know Dr. Rosie O' Rabbit very well. She had seen us through many scratches, scrapes, bumps, and bruises. Though a great doctor, some of the things she said didn't always make sense.

"Top of the morning to you, fellas," Rosie greeted. "Looks like it's going be a fine gathering today."

"Yes it looks like everyone is interested to hear what the Mayor has to say," Sammy replied.

"Well it's like my old dad used to say, 'Whenever you get a lot of animals together like this, you've got yourself a crowd.'" Rosie thought for a moment. "Speaking of crowds, how's your shoulder doing, Sammy? Is it still giving you trouble?"

Sammy and I smiled at each other, remembering when Sammy had hurt himself. "Nope, it feels much better Rosie. Thanks for asking." Sammy moved his arm around in a circle to show her.

Then Rosie looked at me. "And how's that ankle, C.J.? Have you been keeping your weight off of it, like I told you?"

"Yeah, and it feels much better, Rosie" I replied. "Thanks to you. You're a great doctor."

She just smiled proudly.and said

"Well, I do come from a long line of doctors. My old dad taught me everything I know about being a doctor. My uncles were doctors, my cousins were doctors, and my 261 brothers and sisters were all doctors, as well." Rosie paused, staring off into space. "All except for my brother Danny, that is. He's a bit of a strange one. For some reason, he decided to ignore the calling, and devoted his time to a different cause. We are not quite sure why, but for some reason, he just likes to sit up in the top of trees and throw turnips at us." Rosie shook her head back and forth. "Let's just say we don't talk to Danny very much."

As we continued talking to Rosie, the gathering became more and more crowded. Then, suddenly, we heard a chirping sound coming from a cricket Rosie had tied to a string fastened around her waist.

She looked down at the cricket in surprise. "Sorry, fellas, I've got to go; my beeper just went off. Somebody needs some help. Boy, these crickets are amazing aren't they? I guess they can send signals to each other up to five miles away. Wow, Crickets! What will they think of next?"

And just like that, Rosie O'Rabbit was gone.

Looking around, Kip recognized someone else he knew. "Hey look, it's Maggie," he said, pointing behind us.

When I turned around, I saw a very beautiful squirrel with large brown eyes, listening patiently to the complaints of Edna Mouse.

"Who's Maggie?" I asked.

Kip got a big smile on his face and told us that Maggie was the Mayor of Section 6. I could tell by the way she spoke that she was very smart and very strong. Kip went on to explain that Maggie and Nut E. had been friends for a very long time.

"The Mayor tells Maggie things that he doesn't tell anybody else," Kip whispered. "She knows more about him than even I do. If you ask me I think he is in love with her."

"Well, why aren't they together?" I asked.

"I'm not sure," Kip said. "I think the Mayor is waiting to work up the courage to tell Maggie how he feels."

Seeing Kip, Maggie excused herself from Edna and came over to us. Kip introduced us to her, and it wasn't long before I realized that she was a very kind hearted squirrel, and I could tell by the look in her eyes that she was genuinely pleased to meet us.

"Wow, look at this crowd," Maggie commented,

looking around in amazement. "I sure hope I'm going to be able to find a good seat."

"Oh don't worry about that Maggie," Kip said. "The Mayor saved you a seat right up front."

Kid waved us forward. "There's room for you guys up front, too. Come on, follow me."

My heart raced. *This is great,* I thought. *Not only am I going to get to hear the Mayor speak, but I get to be in the front row."* This was one of the best days of my life. Sammy and I were entering the famous Nut E. Squirrel's circle of friends. We were learning secrets about his life, and enjoying some of the privileges that go along with being one of the Mayor's good friends.

As we made our way up towards the front, we heard a loud commotion coming from the back of the clearing. I quickly turned around, and when I did, I saw a group of squirrels pushing their way up through the crowd. The squirrel that seemed to be leading the others was a very angry looking pale gray squirrel. He had dark bags under his eyes, like he hadn't slept in weeks, and a scowl twisted his face. He marched boldly through the crowd, grabbing one animal after another and throwing them to the ground.

"Get out of my way!" he screamed in disgust. "Don't you know who I am?"

The pale gray squirrel walked into the center of the crowd, folded his arms over his chest, and sternly stared up at the podium as his friends all walked up and stood behind him.

"Who is that?" I asked.

Maggie frowned. "That's just mean old Butch. He's the Mayor of the worst section of them all…Section 1. If you ask me, I think he's a little jealous of Nuthaniel's success."

Maggie just ignored Butch, turned around, and walked up to the front row. I was more excited than I had ever been. Today, we were going to hear an actual living legend speak, and I could hardly contain myself. It seemed like forever before Kip finally walked over to the podium, raised his hands up in the air, and quieted the crowd.

"Citizens of Section 7, I know all of you are as excited as I am to hear what the Mayor has to say today. Let me promise you, you won't be disappointed. It is my absolute privilege to introduce perhaps the greatest squirrel that has ever lived. You all know him as the 'legendary squirrel who saved the river.' Ladies and Gentleman, your Mayor . . . the one . . . the only . . . Nuthaniel Eaton Squirrel."

The crowd exploded into cheers as the Mayor entered the clearing. Birds were chirping, children were jumping up and down, and everyone was filled with joy. I was surprised when I first saw him. He was my hero, yet he looked much different than I thought he would. He was an extremely overweight, dark brown squirrel who waddled when he walked, and even though he was smiling, for some reason, his eyes looked sad.

I wasn't sure what to think at first as he began shaking hands with the animals in the front row, but as he reached down and shook my hand, my heart skipped a beat. Then something amazing happened. The Mayor's sad eyes suddenly lit up as he looked over and saw Maggie standing beside us. He smiled from ear to ear as he slowly took her hand, drawing it up towards his lips. He then gently kissed her hand, thanked her for coming, and continued making his way towards the podium.

As he did, a young squirrel rushed forward, "Oh please, Mayor Nuthaniel, can I have your autograph?"

The Mayor just chuckled, said, "Please, son, call me Nut E," and signed his autograph.

When Nut E. finally reached the podium, he raised his hands and silenced the cheering crowd once again. From out of nowhere Edna's voice echoed throughout the clearing. "Abner look how fat he's gotten. He's huge!"

Nut E., trying to pretend like he didn't hear her, quickly started his speech. "My friends, let me start by saying thanks to all of you for coming on such short notice. The reason I have called you here today is to tell you about a monumental construction project that is currently going on right here in Section 7. To my surprise, a team of beavers has taken it upon themselves to build something wonderful right here in our section, and I think that this is a pretty good idea. As we speak, these beavers are diligently working around the clock, constructing something that will change the way we live forever. My friends, you may not realize it, but most of you are prisoners. You are being held captive by the river that divides Section 7 into Tree Ville and Mulberry Meadow. Smaller animals have no way of crossing the river without paying enormous turtle tolls, and that is just not fair. As your Mayor, I refuse to stand here and let this injustice go on any longer"

The crowd cheered as Nut E. furiously pounded his fists down on the podium. I just stood there staring up at this amazing squirrel. As he continued speaking, it became very clear how much he truly cared about the animals that lived in Section 7.

"My friends, I know a lot of you are having trouble affording these outrageous turtle tolls, but thanks to the extraordinary generosity of the beavers, this is all about to change. Now some of you may have already noticed that the beavers have started laying the foundation for a new dam that will span the entire width of the river. This dam will create a walkway that will allow you to freely walk from one side of the river to the other toll-free, and it will be called Beaver Tree Dam."

The crowd roared so loud that I could barely hear myself think. Nut E. slowly raised his hands into the air, and the crowd grew silent once again.

"Ladies and Gentleman, I, too, am thrilled by this news. This dam will put our section head and shoulders above all the other sections up and down the river. No longer will we need Turtle Crossing. Never again will we have to worry about our children washing down river, and my friends, Danger Rapids will be a thing of the past."

The crowd exploded into cheers once again. Even though this new dam wasn't going to affect us butterflies that much, Sammy and I were beginning to get caught up in the excitement of the crowd. Everyone smiled and applauded, everyone that is, except for the pale gray squirrel. He just stood there angrily staring at Nut E. I decided to ignore him, and turned back towards the podium.

"My fellow citizens of Section 7, I am confident that Beaver Tree Dam will set the standard for all future construction projects. We are so fortunate to have something of this magnitude being built right here in our tiny little town. It will be a walkway to a new world, and you small animals will never be held prisoners again. So, let me be the first to welcome you all to a brand new life."

At this point the crowd erupted into a flurry of cheers. The thunderous applause was deafening. Maggie turned to me and said, "Isn't he wonderful. He is such a great squirrel." She gave the Mayor a warm, loving look.

I stood there reveling in the moment, as the Mayor stood behind his podium desperately trying to quiet the excited crowd.

When things had quieted down again, he asked, "Does anyone have any questions?"

"I have a question," someone called from the back of the crowd.

The instant I heard that cold heartless voice it sent a chill down my spine. I recognized it immediately as the voice of my old enemy E. Phil snake. It took a few moments for the crowd to realize who was speaking, but as they turned around they quickly became aware of the danger. All the squirrels in the crowd began to make a high pitched chirping noise, their tails jerking back and forth to create some kind of warning signal. The sound clearly irritated the huge black snake. He clamped his red eyes shut and tilted his head to one side.

"Would you all please stop making that ridiculous noise," E. Phil hissed. "It's driving me crazy. I'm just here as a concerned citizen like everyone else."

The squirrels slowly began to quiet down, and E. Phil continued. "Has anybody thought about what will happen to all that water? Don't you realize that if you dam the river the water will rise up and flood Mulberry Meadow."

E. Phil's words echoed throughout the clearing, and an eerie silence fell over the crowd. What he was saying made a lot of sense. Where would all that water go? I began to think back to what Lewis the turtle had said about the river getting wider, but like the rest of the crowd, I had gotten so caught up into what Nut E. was saying, I never stopped to think what would happen to the river. After a few seconds, a nervous Nut E. squirrel broke through the silence.

"Wa . . . wa . . . uh . . . I don't think that is going to be a problem. Uh . . . uh . . . is it Kip?" Nut E. asked, turning towards his stunned Deputy Mayor.

Kip frantically flipped through his leaf notebook desperately searching for answers as the focus of the crowd shifted to him. He quickly shook his head back and forth, then looked up at Nut E. and shrugged his shoulders.

Nut E. gave a worried grin as he turned back towards

the crowd. "This is preposterous. Mulberry Meadow is not going to flood. I'm sure the beavers have explored all the possible dangers associated with this project. Why on earth would you say something like that?"

"Because I was just there," E. Phil answered. "The meadow started flooding a few minutes ago."

Suddenly, Edna mouse spoke up. "Why should we believe you?" She scowled at E. Phil. "You're nothing but a lying, slimy snake."

The rest of the crowd joined in, defending Nut E. against E. Phil.

Seeming to realize he was losing control of the meeting, Nut E. quickly spoke again. "Listen, my friends," Nut E. said calmly. "Don't let this snake talk you into believing something that is simply not true."

E. Phil just threw his head back and laughed. "You lie very well, Nut E., but I suspect that you have some personal reason for allowing the beavers to build this dam. After all, there are nuts to be had, Mr. Mayor, and it looks to me like you are gaining weight."

Hearing this, Edna put her hands on her hips and stomped her foot on the ground. "Are you accusing the Mayor of taking bribes? I have never heard such a ridiculous accusation in all my life. How dare you question the squirrel who saved the river? Mayor Nut E. Squirrel has done more for Section 7 then all the other Mayors before him put together. You, sir, are despicable!"

E. Phil slowly brought his head down until he was face to face with Edna mouse. "You know Edna," E. Phil said in a slow, soft voice, "I've been noticing that for some reason you seem to be in a particularly bad mood this morning. And I have to ask, what is eating you? Oh yes, that's right . . . I am."

Without warning, E. Phil's tongue shot out, grabbed Edna, and pulled her into his mouth. Immediately, the squirrels began chirping loudly once again. After a few seconds, E. Phil closed his eyes, painfully shook his head back and forth, and slowly spit out a wet, dazed and finally silenced Edna mouse. As she laid there gasping for air, E. Phil spoke again.

"I can not stand that hideous noise," he hissed. "Would you please stop?"

Rosie O'Rabbit rushed over to help the disoriented mouse. Edna looked up at her with frightened eyes. "I nearly died," she gasped. "I nearly started my Life Watch."

Unable to withstand the constant high pitched chirping any longer, E. Phil decided to leave. "This meeting has left a bad taste in my mouth," E. Phil groaned. "If you animals want to drown, that's up to you. I'm probably going to leave the meadow, anyway. So I don't really care."

As E. Phil slithered off, he turned back to the crowd one last time. "I hope that everybody here can swim."

I was in shock at that moment. I didn't know what to believe, but then I heard an angry voice coming from the center of the crowd. Looking back, I saw Butch glaring at the Mayor.

"Is what the snake said true, Nut E.? Is Mulberry

Meadow flooding?" Butch asked.

"Well . . . uh . . . I don't think so," Nut E. stuttered.

"You don't *think*," Butch challenged. "Have you checked?"

Nut E. nervously fidgeted around trying to regain his composure. "Well, no, Butch," he admitted. "I didn't . . . I . . . I don't have the time to check into every ridiculous accusation that comes along."

"Well somebody needs to check into it!" Butch screamed.

Maggie bristled with anger, and could not stay quiet any longer. "Listen, Butch, what are you yelling at him for? He's not the one building the dam, the beavers are. So why don't you just leave him alone!"

Butch just pointed towards Nut E. "He is responsible for everything that goes on in Section 7. He is the Mayor. If he can't do the job, than maybe we should get someone who can."

"This is ridiculous!" Nut E. yelled. "Section 7 does not have a flooding problem. That dam is not hurting anyone. And I will not stand here and listen to this nonsense any longer. This meeting is over!"

With that, Nut E. turned away from the podium and stepped into a large puddle of water, sinking to his waist.

Seeing this, Butch turned towards the crowd and yelled "That's it! Just because your Mayor has chosen to turn his back on this terrible problem, doesn't mean that I'm going to. Someone needs to save Section 7 from those beavers, and it looks like it is going to be me. I'm going over to Mulberry Meadow to check on this situation right now. Who's coming with me?"

Several worried members of the crowd joined Butch and his friends, and began heading off towards Mulberry Meadow.

Suddenly, Sammy turned to me with a terrified look on his face. "C.J., what about our eggs?"

The full weight of what Sammy had just said hit me all at once. I hadn't thought about our eggs. But if what E. Phil said was true, and the meadow really was flooding, our eggs were in grave danger. Sammy immediately leapt into the air, and I quickly followed after him. I had never seen Sammy fly as fast as he did that morning. We were in Mulberry Meadow within minutes, and as we flew in and landed on the branches of the Mulberry Bush, we could see that the meadow had started to flood just as E. Phil had said.

"What are we going to do Sammy?" I asked.

Sammy desperately looked around. "I don't know, C.J." Sammy said trying to remain calm. "But luckily since the eggs are so high up in the Mulberry Bush we have some time. It will take a while for the water to reach them."

"Can't we just move them?" I asked desperately trying to think of something.

"I wish we could, C.J., but they're too fragile. They are going to have to stay where they are.

"But Sammy, if we don't do something soon, our eggs will drown."

Sammy stood staring at the eggs. I felt an unbelievably

helpless feeling in the pit of my stomach as I stared down at my future child. All the adventures that I had planned for him seemed to be slipping away.

"There's got to be something we can do, Sammy."

Just then, I heard a voice off in the distance. Butch, the angry squirrel from the meeting, tromped through the muddy water slowly covering the meadow. A large group of other animals followed closely behind him.

"Hey, what's going on over there?" Butch yelled.

I raced over to Butch as quickly as I could. "Sir, you have to help us," I pleaded. "The meadow is flooding, and our eggs are going to drown."

Butch stopped and looked around at the crowd following him. He cleared his throat and spoke loud enough for everyone to hear. "Don't worry, my friend, I won't let your eggs drown. You have my word on that."

I felt a little relieved, but I was still worried. "Well what are we going to do?" I asked.

Butch put his hand on my shoulder and said, "We've just got to find a way to get the beavers to stop building that dam."

That's it! I thought to myself. *The beavers. We need to go talk to the beavers. Once they hear about our eggs, they will stop building the dam for sure.*

"Thank you, sir, thank you," I said, shaking Butch's hand. "Come on, Sammy, let's go! We've got to talk to the beavers!"

Butch and the others began trudging through the mud again as Sammy and I raced off towards Beaver Tree Dam.

Many thoughts raced through my head: *We've got to stop the beavers; We are the only two butterflies left in the meadow, and it is up to us to not only save our own eggs, but the eggs of every butterfly in the Mulberry Bush.*

I knew at that moment we didn't have much time left before we had to migrate, but in that short space of time, we would have to find a way to stop that dam from being built, or the world we once knew would no longer exist.

When we arrived at Beaver Tree Dam, I couldn't believe my eyes. It was huge! It was hard to imagine that these little animals could construct something as monstrous as this dam. Even though it was only half way done, just looking at it took my breath away. The beavers ran around everywhere, working very hard and very fast. We discovered that the leader of the project was a very well built beaver named Jackhammer. He wore half of a grapefruit peel as a construction helmet, had a gnawed pencil behind his ear, and carried a tree bark clipboard. We approached him and hurriedly introduced ourselves. Sammy then told him about the problem with our eggs, and that the Meadow had started to flood.

"Of course the meadow is flooding." Jackhammer replied. "The water's got to go somewhere. What were you expecting?"

I could tell Jackhammer was a very busy beaver and that he had little interest in what we had to say.

"You mean you already knew about this problem?" Sammy asked amazed.

At that point, Jackhammer turned to one of the other

beavers, and yelled, Okay, Chainsaw, lets get this tree down."

The beaver he called Chainsaw had huge, sharp front teeth. Without hesitation, Chainsaw began gnawing away at the tree that Jackhammer pointed to. He chewed through the tree so quickly that wood chips flew all around him. Then, suddenly, he stopped and yelled: "Timber!" With a slight push, the tree fell, shaking the ground as it came crashing down.

"But Jackhammer, you don't understand," Sammy pleaded. "If the meadow continues to flood, we will lose our eggs, and there will be no more caterpillars in Mulberry Meadow."

"Listen, buddy," Jackhammer replied still too busy to look at us. "I can appreciate your problem, but we have families to feed too."

Noticing a beaver with a very strong and flat tail, Jackhammer got an angry look on his face and yelled, "Forklift, what are you waiting for? That log's not going to move itself."

The beaver named Forklift immediately turned around and began backing up towards the log. As he lowered his tail to the ground, he began making a beeping sound.

"Beep . . . Beep . . . Beep," he warned, as he wedged his tail under the log and lifted it into the air. Then he carried the log over to the river and dumped it into the water.

"Look, fellas," Jackhammer said to us. "I'd love to

help you, but I can't. I don't have the authority to stop construction of the dam. If I could, I would. But I can't. I'm sorry." He looked away again. "Rutter, get on that log and bring it down here. I want to get this one in place before lunch."

Standing on top of the log, Rutter stuck his tail in the water and used it to steer the tree downriver. When he reached the dam, he turned the log sideways and guided it into position, where he held it long enough for another beaver named Mason to pack mud around it, cementing the log in place. As Sammy and I watched the beavers build the dam, we realized that if we didn't act fast, the dam was going to be finished soon and it would be too late.

"What do you mean you don't have the authority?" Sammy asked. "Aren't you the one in charge here?"

For the first time all day, Jackhammer looked directly at us and said, "Listen, Buddy, if you want to stop the dam from being built than you need to talk to the guy that hired us."

Sammy and I looked at each other, confused.

"Wait a minute," Sammy said. "I thought that building this dam was your idea."

"Oh, no," Jackhammer said. "You've got it all wrong. We were hired to build the dam."

I began to feel nervous.

"Well, um . . . who hired you?" I asked.

"Don't you know?" he said, shaking his head back and forth. "It was the Mayor. It was Nut E. Squirrel. He's the one who hired us."

At that moment, it felt like someone had just punched me in the stomach. I felt dizzy, and I couldn't breathe. I couldn't believe what I was hearing. The squirrel that I had idolized, the one I had looked up to ever since I had become a butterfly, was the one responsible for possibly destroying our eggs. I staggered backwards, trying to keep my balance, but it was no use. I began to fall. When I did, someone caught me and lifted me back up onto my feet. I shook my head, trying to clear my eyes, and noticed that it was Butch who was holding me up.

"It's Nut E. Squirrel," I gasped. "He's the one that is responsible for this. He hired the beavers. It's . . . it's his fault."

Butch smiled darkly as he looked at me and whispered, "Oh thank you." Then he pulled back away from me, and turned to face the awaiting crowd. When he did this, my body crumpled, and I fell to the ground. "Did you hear that?" Butch screamed. "Nut E. Squirrel is killing the butterfly eggs. That's it! I've heard enough! I tried to tell you people that he was no good, but no one would believe me. Well, they are going to believe me now. Come on, let's go to his office. Mayor Nut E. Squirrel has got some explaining to do."

As the angry crowd headed off towards Nut E.'s office, Sammy slowly walked over and lifted me back onto my feet.

"Hey, C.J.," Sammy said softly, "I'm sorry. I know he was your hero, and I know you are pretty upset right now, but you have got to pull yourself together. Our children are in danger, and they need us to be strong. So, come on, let's go. We are going to have a little chat with Mayor Nut E. Squirrel."

The Promise

I was still in a daze as Sammy and I flew towards the Mayor's office over in Tree Ville. We knew that we had to find some way to convince him that the meadow was flooding and that he had to stop the beavers from building the dam. As we flew higher into the air, I could see the angry crowd below us. Butch and his friends were crossing the river at Tree Top Gap. Tree Top Gap was made up of two large oak trees that were on opposite sides of the river. They were directly across from each other and each tree had a limb that stretched out over the water leaving a large gap between them. I watched, as each squirrel jumped from one branch to the other landing safely on the other side. We flew ahead of the crowd, and as we neared the Mayor's office, I was angry and disappointed. I wasn't sure what I was going to say to him. I felt like he had let me down. When we arrived there, we realized that the Mayor's office was inside the top of a large hollowed out tree near the river on the edge of Tree Ville. Inside, there were two rooms: Kip's office, and beyond that the office of Mayor Nut E. Squirrel. When we walked in, Kip was pacing back and forth, mumbling to himself.

"Where's the Mayor Kip?" Sammy shouted. "We need to speak with him!"

Kip just threw up his hands. "Please fellas," he pleaded. "This is not a good time. The Mayor has had a tough day. This whole Beaver Tree Dam thing is a huge mess. At this point, we are just trying to sort things out. Right now, the Mayor is in an important meeting, and I'm afraid you are not going to be able to see him today."

Sammy was angrier now than ever. "We need to see the Mayor, Kip!" Sammy demanded. "Our eggs are in danger!"

As Sammy explained to Kip all about the trouble with our eggs, I quietly walked over to the leaf curtain which separated Nut E.'s office from Kip's. I slowly peeled back the leaf, and peeked inside. Nut E. was sitting at his desk, talking to Maggie as he nervously shoved one nut after another into his mouth.

"I don't understand, Maggie," Nut E. said in a worried voice. "This dam is going to be a great thing for Section 7. Animals are finally going to be able to cross the river without having to pay such outrageous turtle tolls. I mean, so what if there is a little extra water over in Mulberry Meadow. It's not hurting anyone."

As I heard these words, my anger slowly began to fade. I realized the Mayor wasn't trying to hurt our eggs, he just didn't understand what was really going on. Nut E. still looked a little shaken as Maggie gently reached over and took his hand.

"Nuthaniel, I know you are just trying to help the smaller animals who are too little to cross at Tree Top Gap," she said. "And I admire you for that. But if what they're saying is true, and Mulberry Meadow really is flooding, then I think you need to find a better way."

Nut E. rubbed his tired eyes, and sighed heavily. "Oh Maggie, I don't understand how all this got so out of control. When I hired the beavers to build the dam, they never said anything about flooding."

Maggie shook her head in surprise. "You hired the beavers?" she asked.

Just then, something crashed behind me. Before I could turn around to see what it was, someone grabbed me by the shoulders and lifted me up off the ground. I was pushed forward straight through the leaf curtain, past Nut E.'s desk, and held hanging in mid air face to face with the Mayor.

"Tell him what you just told me!" Butch scowled as he pushed me even closer to Nut E.'s face.

Nut E. looked shocked as I stared into his eyes trying to make sense of what had just happened.

"What's going on here?" Nut E. demanded.

Butch just shook me back and forth, and said, "Go ahead, butterfly. Tell him!"

Nut E. looked at me confused as I stuttered desperately trying to find the right words. "You . . . you . . . you are the one that hired the beavers?"

Nut E. thought for a moment, and then quickly began defending himself. "Well, of course I did, son, the beavers aren't going to work for free."

"But sir," I said, "Beaver Tree Dam is causing Mulberry Meadow to flood."

Nut E. tapped his foot impatiently. "I'm aware of that," he said. "But I don't see how a little bit of water is going to hurt anything. This dam is a great thing. It is going to help everyone."

"But Mr. Mayor, you don't understand. Our eggs are over there. If the meadow continues to flood, they will drown."

Nut E. looked down and shook his head back and forth. With that, Butch carelessly tossed me aside. I bounced off the wall and landed hard on the floor. I was beginning to realize that Butch was not a very nice squirrel. He had used me to humiliate Nut E. and make himself look good in front of the crowd. I glared up at him. Ignoring me, Butch turned back towards Nut E.

"Nut E.," Butch screamed. "You have finally gone too far. This dam of yours is going to flood us all. You are a fool, and I am going to show everyone what a horrible Mayor you truly are."

Just then, Maggie stepped forward and began defending Nut E.

"That isn't fair, Butch," Maggie said. "So maybe he did hire the beavers, but he was just trying to help the smaller animals live better lives. That's what a Mayor is supposed to do."

Butch shot Maggie a harsh stare. "He doesn't care about the smaller animals," Butch argued. "He's just doing it to make himself look good."

"Now slow down there a minute, Butch," Nut E. interrupted. "I'll admit that the dam has a few minor problems—"

"Minor problems!" Butch screamed. "Mulberry Meadow is under water. Come with me right now. Let's go over there, and you can see for yourself the damage you are causing."

Nut E. thought for a moment, nervously looked around, and said, "That's okay. I . . . I . . . I'll just take your word for it."

This made Butch even madder. "No!" he shouted "You need to see this for yourself. Come on, let's go! Right now!"

I didn't know what to think as I watched the Mayor grow more and more nervous. He quickly pulled another nut from his desk and began devouring it.

"This is ridiculous," he said, as little pieces of the nut flew out from the sides of his mouth. "That dam needs to be built. I'm sure we can work all these problems out in due time. But for right now, those beavers aren't hurting anyone."

At that point, I heard a familiar voice. "Tiiiiimmmber," Chainsaw the beaver yelled from down below.

Suddenly, the tree we were all standing in began to fall. The whole room shifted to one side, and when it did, everything in the office slid across the floor. Maggie started screaming as pictures flew off the walls, and the desk flipped over on its side. It took every ounce of my flying skills to lift myself up into the air and avoid being crushed by a huge wooden filing cabinet that crashed into the wall where I'd been standing. Nut E. reached out, grabbed onto Maggie, and held her close. When the tree finally hit the ground, Nut E.'s body crashed hard against the ground cushioning Maggie's fall. Everybody remained silent for several moments. As the dust began to settle, Butch crawled out from under a large pile of nuts that had spilled out of the closet.

"Is everybody all right?" Sammy yelled from the other room.

Realizing that no one was seriously hurt, we all began to slowly make our way out of the fallen tree. A few of the animals from the angry crowd helped us out of the door. When I flew out into the sunlight, Kip was brushing himself off, and yelling at Chainsaw. Chainsaw just shrugged his shoulders, said "oops," and ran off.

Butch began to tremble with anger. "This is exactly what I was talking about! Butch screamed. "Those beavers are a menace! And you were the one that hired them!" Butch continued to yell at Nut E. as Maggie struggled to pull him out of the office door. "I don't think you realize how much damage those beavers are causing. That's why we're all going to Mulberry Meadow right now."

Still trying to free himself from the fallen tree, Nut E. became angry. "Butch, I'm not going over to Mulberry Meadow with you!"

"Why?" Butch scowled as he pointed towards the crowd. "Are you afraid to show these people what's really going on over there?"

"No . . . No, it's just—"

"It's just what?" Butch interrupted. "It will take us ten minutes. We will run over to Tree Top Gap real quick, jump across, and . . ."

At that moment, Butch stopped talking. He thought for a moment, and as he watched Nut E. still struggling to drag his overweight body through the door, he slowly began to smile.

"That's it," he said triumphantly. "You *can't* get over to Mulberry Meadow, can you? With that overweight body of yours, you couldn't possibly cross Tree Top Gap. That's why you are building the dam." Butch began laughing. "You're not trying to help the little animals get across the river; you're trying to help one big one. You hear that, ladies and gentleman?" Butch said, turning towards the crowd. "Nut E. Squirrel is building this dam for his own personal gain. Because he is too fat to cross the river, we all have to suffer."

As Butch said this, I didn't know what to think. *"Could this be true? I thought to myself. Is Nut E. Squirrel really building this dam just so HE can get across the river?*

51

The crowd stood there in silence, staring at Nut E. as Maggie finally pulled him free of the doorway and back onto his feet.

Maggie was furious.

"That's insane Butch," she said. "Nut E. Squirrel is a hero, and when your incompetence threatened the river, it was Nut E. that saved us all. You're just jealous because he made you look bad. You should be ashamed of yourself for even suggesting such a ridiculous accusation. Of course Nut E. can get across the river." Maggie looked over at Nut E., then up towards Tree Top Gap. "He may not be able to jump across Tree Top Gap like the rest of us, but he certainly can use Turtle Crossing."

Butch smiled. "I don't think so," he said confidently. "I think he's too fat."

"No he's not" Maggie shot back.

"Oh really? Then let's find out. What are we waiting for? Let's all go to Turtle Crossing."

As I looked over at Nut E., I saw doubt in his eyes. He looked very nervous, and I could tell that the last place he wanted to go was Turtle Crossing. But not wanting to disappoint Maggie, or the crowd, he reluctantly followed the other squirrels toward the river. Sammy and I followed after them. I was still very worried about our eggs, but I was pretty sure that everything was going to be resolved fairly soon. When we arrived at Turtle Crossing, Lewis the turtle was waiting for us.

"Okay, Nut E.," Butch sneered, "here is your chance to prove me wrong."

Nut E. looked very nervous as he spoke.

"I don't see why I have to prove anything to you, Butch," the Mayor said defiantly.

Maggie walked over to Nut E. and put her arm around him. "I agree with you, Nuthaniel." Maggie said. " You shouldn't have to prove anything to him. But it will only take a moment and then he will have to leave you alone."

"She's right," Butch said confidently. "The minute you get across that river, I won't say another word."

Nut E. hesitated for a while, but then he finally built up enough courage and agreed to take the ride.

However, when Lewis turned around and saw Nut E., he said, "That load is going to cost you extra."

"What? This is outrageous," Nut E. complained. "I am not going to pay extra to get across this river."

"Don't worry about it. Allow me," Butch said, smiling as he paid Lewis the turtle tolls.

Running out of excuses, Nut E. had no choice but to get on Lewis's back. He looked over at the crowd, paused for a moment, and then gently put his right foot on the turtle's shell. Then he slowly shifted his weight and lifted his left foot off the shore. When he did this, the turtle instantly sank straight to the bottom leaving Nut E. up to his waist in water. He was still standing on the turtle's back and he had an embarrassed look on his face.

After a few seconds, an air bubble slowly rose to the surface and popped. From it, we heard Lewis's voice shout the word: "Get!" It was soon followed by a second air bubble, and when it popped, we heard Lewis yell: "Off!"

Nut E. slowly stepped off of the turtle's back, and Lewis shot up like a rocket out of the water and flew through the air. When he landed on the shore he was flat on his back, and laid there gasping for air.

Just then, out of nowhere, Peety the chipmunk came running up next to Lewis and said: "Now that's a back flip." Peety patted Lewis on the stomach and smiled. "I'm glad to see you are finally on board, son. But it's too late. Entirely too late. I have already started working on my flying machine, and when it's done, I'm afraid you turtles might be out of a job. So, like I said, it's too late. Because not only will I be able to fly over my domain as the acting Owl, but I will also be able to give animals rides across the river. Things are about to change around here, yes indeed, things are about to change."

As fast as Peety had come, he was gone. And as Nut E. crawled out of the water, Butch, his friends, and the rest of the crowd started laughing at him. Maggie was shocked and Nut E. was humiliated.

"I told you he was too fat to cross the river," Butch said proudly. "That's the reason he's building the dam."

Trying to save whatever shred of dignity that he had left, Nut E. quickly yelled

"Whether I can use Turtle Crossing or not doesn't change the fact that I am building this dam for the betterment of Section 7."

"Listen, Nut Eater!" Butch threatened. "If you're too fat to get across the river, then you shouldn't be in charge. The animals that live over in Mulberry Meadow deserve a Mayor that can get across Tree Top Gap, and come visit them every once in awhile. I am going to start the process to have you removed, and soon I will take my place back as the rightful leader." Butch looked at his friends, and said, "Come on, boys, let's go across Tree Top Gap like real squirrels."

Before he left, Butch turned back towards Nut E. and said, "I will see you on the other side . . . oh, wait . . . no I won't." Butch and his friends laughed as they left turtle crossing.

At that moment, I didn't know what to think. *"Could this be true?"* I thought to myself. *"Could my hero really be this selfish?"* There was a lot of whispering going on as the rest of the crowd slowly began walking away in disgust. After they were gone, Nut E. reluctantly turned around and faced a disappointed Maggie.

Her eyes welled up with tears. "How could you do this to me? I defended you."

Nut E. tried to say something, but she ignored him and continued to speak.

"Butch was right. You can't cross the river." Maggie shook her head. "You *ARE* building this dam for your own personal gain. Don't you understand, you're not helping Section 7, you're hurting it. If you're building this dam just so you can get across the river then you need to find another way."

Fighting back the tears, Maggie turned to go.

"Maggie, wait," Nut E., pleaded, desperately trying to keep her from leaving.

She stopped and slowly turned back towards Nut E. "What?"

With shame in his voice, Nut E. quietly said, "I'm sorry."

Maggie's face softened. "Nuthaniel, this dam is a bad thing. You saved the entire river once. I'm begging you, please save it again." When Maggie left, Nut E. looked devastated. I couldn't help but feel sorry for the Mayor.

At that moment, we heard Butch and his friends off in the distance. They were crossing Tree Top Gap one after another. As Butch landed on the other side, he looked down at Nut E. and yelled, "So long, tubby!"

All of Butch's friends laughed as Nut E. lowered his head in shame. As I stared at the humiliated Nut E. Squirrel, anger began to build up inside of me. I realized that Butch was making fun of Nut E. just to make himself look better, but it actually made Butch look like an idiot. It was then that I realized that animals who make fun of other animals just because they are different are really just sad themselves and not very self-confident. Even though the Mayor was overweight, it didn't give Butch the right to make fun of him.

When Sammy heard this, he looked over at Kip and asked

"What's Butch's problem anyway?" Sammy asked. "Why does he hate the Mayor so much?"

"Oh, it's a long story," Kip began. As he started telling us the story between Nut E. and Butch, I noticed that the Mayor was not even listening. He just sat there blankly staring out over the river. Nut E. was very sad, and he looked humiliated.

"Butch has hated the Mayor for a long time," Kip explained. "And he would love nothing more than to see the Mayor removed from office."

"Why?" Sammy asked. "I thought everybody liked Nut E."

"Most animals do," Kip said. "But you see, Butch used to be the Mayor of Section 7"

This surprised me.

"He was?" I asked. "I didn't know that."

"Yes, he was." Kip said. "But he wasn't a very good Mayor. So when Nut E. ran against him four years ago, he beat Butch by a landslide. Butch was forced to leave Section 7 and eventually went on to become the Mayor of Section 1, mostly because nobody else wanted the job. You see, Section 1 is the worst section of them all. The river bed there is littered with garbage, and almost no one lives there."

"But that's not all," Kip continued. "It gets worse. About two years ago, all the animals up and down the river began to get very sick, and none of the baby fish were hatching. Everyone was afraid that we would have to abandon the river forever. But it was Nut E. who figured out that something was poisoning the water. He decided to walk the entire length of the river until he finally found the problem. And he did. He discovered that someone had thrown an old paint can into the river, and the paint was polluting the water."

"Oh, yeah, I heard something about that," I said, excited. "Isn't that when everybody started calling him the squirrel that saved the river?"

"Yes," Kip said. "But the problem was that he found the can in Section 1, right under Butch's nose. Butch was humiliated, and swore that he would get back at the Mayor someday."

Kip stopped talking and slowly lowered his head. "I guess today he has."

Then Kip stared straight into my eyes, and said, "If only you would have just come to us first. I'm sure we could have solved your problem without involving Butch."

Kip shook his head, turned around, and walked back towards Nut E. Sammy and I just stood there not knowing what to say.

What have I done? I thought to myself. *In one day, I have managed to ruin the career of probably the greatest squirrel that has ever lived. Instead of giving him the benefit of the doubt, I flew off the handle and blamed him for something that he really wasn't responsible for. He didn't know our eggs were going to be in danger. If I would have just told him about the problem, I'm sure he would have fixed it. Instead I went to Butch, and gave him everything he needed to bring down the Mayor.*

I felt horrible, but I was about to feel worse.

"What are we going to do now, Mr. Mayor?" Kip asked Nut E.

Nut E. just took a deep breath. "The only thing we can do, Kip. We've got to stop building the dam."

As Nut E. said this, he looked sadder than ever. "I never meant to hurt anybody," he whispered.

Kip got a worried look on his face. "But sir, you can't stop the dam. You have got to get across that river. These animals don't know how important it is for you to get over there. What about—"

"I know," Nut E. interrupted. "But right now the future of Section 7 is more important than my personal needs. Maybe I can find some other way to cross."

"But Mr. Mayor," Kip argued. "I can't let you do this. It's too important."

Nut E. just put his hand on Kip's shoulder. "Kip, let it go. It's . . . it's over."

Kip lowered his head in defeat as Nut E. continued.

"So please, Kip, go tell the beavers to stop building the dam."

Kip nodded his head and reluctantly left for Beaver Tree Dam. I felt worse, now, than ever before. It was amazing how quickly things had changed. The day had started out so full of hope, but now there was nothing left but sorrow. At that point, Sammy flew up next to me. "Boy, C.J., do you feel as bad as I do?"

I nodded as I stared at Nut E.

"Well, at least our eggs are safe," he said, trying to cheer me up.

I turned to face Sammy. "Yeah, they are, but at what cost. We've ruined the life of a legend. In one day, we managed to humiliate Nut E. in front of everyone. The girl he loves won't even speak to him. He is probably going to be removed from office. And it's all our fault."

"Well, not everything was our fault," Sammy said.

"Yes, I know Sammy, but we've still got to do something about it. We've got to at least try to help the Mayor."

Sammy looked confused.

"What can we do?" Sammy asked.

I thought for a moment. Then, it hit me. "We need to get him across the river, Sammy. If we can do that, everything will be all right."

"But how are we going to get him across the river, C.J.?" Sammy asked. "He's too heavy to take Turtle Crossing, and he's too fat to jump across Tree Top Gap."

"That's it, Sammy!" I exclaimed. "We just need to get him to lose some weight. Then he'll be able to get across the river like the other squirrels."

Sammy looked concerned.

"C.J., we don't have a whole lot of time. We have to go to Butterfly Island before it snows. Remember, butterflies can't fly in the snow."

"I know, Sammy, but it's like you said, we've got at least three weeks before we have to leave."

Sammy looked a little disappointed.

"Well...so much for finding new adventures."

"Ahh, Sammy, don't you understand. This is the adventure we were looking for. Maybe helping someone else is the greatest adventure of them all."

Sammy thought for a moment. "You're right, C.J. We

can do this. If he loses a little weight, we can get the Mayor across the river."

Hearing Sammy say this made me feel better. Sammy and I quickly flew over to the Mayor. "Excuse us, Mr. Mayor, we want to apologize for all the trouble we have caused you."

Nut E. just shook his head. "Oh no, son. It's not your fault. I was so busy trying to cross the river that I didn't take the time to think about all the problems the dam could cause. I guess I don't deserve to be Mayor."

"Listen, Sir, Sammy and I have got it all figured out. All we've got to do is prove that you can get across the river, and everybody will forget all about Butch and Beaver Tree Dam."

The Mayor thought for a moment.

"Well I do need to get over there," he said. "But how? How am I going to do that?"

"We've been thinking about it," I replied. "And we decided that if you are willing to lose a little bit of weight, Sammy and I will help you get across the river."

"I don't know, fellas. I've tried to lose weight before, and it never seems to work out. I just can't do it."

"That doesn't sound like the Mayor I know. The Mayor I know saved an entire river once all by himself. You weren't afraid to try then, and I don't understand why you are afraid now."

Becoming excited, Sammy jumped in. "Mr. Mayor, there is nothing to be afraid of. You see, my friend C.J. and I are expert adventurers. We have been climbing rocks and trees since the day we were born. And I know for a fact that if you are willing to do a little bit of training, we can help you get across Tree Top Gap."

As Sammy and I continued to encourage the Mayor, his sadness was slowly replaced by a look of determination. "Maybe I can do this," he said. "After all, what do I have to lose?"

I smiled when I heard this.

"Now that's the legendary Nut E. Squirrel I know," I said proudly.

Nut E. stood up, brushed himself off, and looked around. "Lose weight, huh? I can do that. I just might need a little help. Kip, take a note. Get me the best weight loss specialists in the area. Spare no expense, this is important."

It was at that point that Nut E. realized Kip wasn't there. "Oh, that's right," he said. "I sent him to stop the dam."

But Nut E.'s determination held strong, and he looked at us confidently. "You know what? I am going to need some volunteers to be in charge of a very special project. This will be one of the most important projects in the history of Section 7. Everything I am able to do to help this town from now on will depend on the success of this mission. If you two chose to accept this mission, your lives will be forever linked with mine. You will be in charge of everyone and everything related to my weight loss, and eventually my crossing of the river. I will need your complete attention and focus. You will go everywhere

I go, and will do everything I do. In the end, you will have served Mulberry Meadow more than any other butterflies who have ever lived."

I was so excited I could hardly breathe, and I could tell Sammy was starting to get excited as well

"We'll do it!" I yelled.

Nut E. smiled. "Good, then let's get started. From now on, you two will have official positions with the Mayor's Office."

My heart welled up with pride as he said this. "Did you hear that, Sammy? We are going to be special assistants to the Mayor."

"Maybe you're right, C.J," he said, smiling proudly. "Perhaps this is the adventure we were looking for."

The Quick Fix

Kip did everything the Mayor told him to do. He stopped the beavers from building the dam, and they moved on to another project. Most importantly, the water stopped rising and our eggs were safe. Nut E. had helped us, and now it was our turn to return the favor. From that moment on, we never left the Mayor's side. Sammy and I had risen to very important butterflies over night. It was a little scary, but I loved it. Not only did we get to hang out with the world famous Nut E. Squirrel, but he was depending on us to save his career.

That night we told Kip to spread the word that Mayor Nut E. Squirrel needed help to lose weight fast. We weren't sure if anybody would respond, but we soon found out that word travels fast along the river. When we arrived at Nut E.'s office the next morning, which was still lying on its' side, we were surprised to see a huge crowd of animals waiting for us. Kip was running around scribbling names down on his clipboard. It seemed like every self-proclaimed weight loss specialist in the world was there. Nut E. sat in a chair on the ground out in front of his office. He had his legs crossed, and had a big pile of nuts stacked up beside him. One after another he ate the nuts as he watched Kip frantically running around in circles trying to maintain some sort of order. We hoped these animals would be able to help Nut E., but as Kip introduced each of them, our hopes quickly faded.

The first one, a raccoon named Shifty, slowly walked up to Nut E.'s side and cautiously looked around. He kept looking over his shoulder to make sure nobody was watching him. Then, when he was sure the coast was clear, he slowly reached in to the fur under his arm and pulled out a handful of small pills.

"Pssst . . . hey, buddy," Shifty whispered. "I hear you need to lose some weight quick."

He looked over his shoulder once again, and handed Nut E. one of the pills. "Here, take this Rid-O-Fat pill," Shifty said. "This will take care of your weight problem in no time."

Nut E. took the pill and swallowed it as Shifty continued. "Now, I should probably tell you there *ARE* a few side effects. This pill has been known to cause drowsiness, dizziness, headaches, blindness, deafness, heart failure, kidney disease, acne, gingivitis, and paranoia. Oh yeah, and excessive itching."

By the time Shifty finished speaking, Nut E. was scratching himself uncontrollably. Kip immediately turned to the crowd and yelled: "Next!"

That is when a short, little Chinese porcupine walked up and stood in front of Nut E. He put his hands together, palm to palm, and bowed. "Hello, my name is Pin Quill. I will help you lose weight fast, using something I call acupuncture."

Without warning, the porcupine reached over his shoulder pulled several quills out of his back, and threw them at Nut E.

"Agh," Nut E. whimpered, as seven quills hit him in the stomach like darts.

Seeing this, Kip raced to Nut E.'s side and began pulling the quills out of his stomach. *This is going to be a lot harder than we were expecting* I thought to myself. Just then we heard a familiar voice.

"Would you like a hot, chewy, gooey, juicy, candy apple on a stick?"

It was Telly Vision and he was selling candy apples.

"If you do, come quick. You don't have to buy, you just gotta try a little lick of this candied apple on a stick."

I could tell by the look on Nut E.'s face that he was happy to see him. "Telly," Nut E. said smiling. "I'm glad to see you. Give me one of those apples. All this losing weight stuff has made me hungry."

Nut E. grabbed the candied apple and started eating it. As he did an anteater named Art Vark made his way up to Nut E. and said: "Why spend countless hours dieting and exercising? There is a much easier way to lose weight my friend, and I'm here to show you how. It is a simple procedure called liposuction. What we do is vacuum the fat right out of your body. Here, let me demonstrate."

Suddenly, the anteater plunged his snout into Nut E.'s candied apple, and sucked out all the insides, leaving the Mayor holding nothing but a shriveled peel on a stick. Nut E. was so shocked by what he had just seen that his mouth dropped open, and pieces of chewed apple fell out onto the ground.

"Okay," Kip said. "We'll aahhh . . . we'll get back to you."

As the day went on, Sammy and I began to feel more and more sorry for Nut E. None of the animals that he had met seemed to be able to help him. But the Mayor didn't give up trying.

"Good day, mates," the next specialist said, introducing himself to us. He was a koala bear, and spoke with an Australian accent. "My name is Sydney, and I'm from down unda," the koala said. "Now what I'm about to show you is cutting edge technology. This technique has never been properly tested nor approved by anyone other than myself."

Sydney slowly pulled two electric eels out of a bag and held them by their tails.

"Now look at these two beauties," he said with an

excited smile on his face. "They're capable of administering a shock of up to five hundred volts each. Here let me show ya, grab one of those nuts and try and eat it."

As Nut E. popped the nut into his mouth, Sydney whipped the eels at him and when he did they both uncoiled and bit into Nut E.'s body. Nut E. painfully shook back and forth, and his teeth clinched together as the electricity raced through him.

"Now a jolt like this," Sydney explained, "would surely kill most smaller animals. But with your weight and body size you should be all right. I call this shock therapy, and after a few weeks of this treatment you'll never want to eat again."

Smoke poured from Nut E.'s body, and his fur stood on end.

"Oh, for the love of The Owl!" Nut E. screamed. "Get them off of me!"

It took Nut E. a while to recover, but he finally worked up enough courage to continue and reluctantly asked to see the next candidate. The next candidate was a huge gray possum named Awesommus Possumus.

"The best way to lose weight is to sweat it off," he said in a very deep voice rubbing his belly. "And I happen to have a built in sweat box, right here."

Awesommus didn't waste any time. He grabbed Nut E., lifted him off the ground, and shoved him into his pouch. When Sammy and I heard Nut E.'s muffled cries coming from the possum's stomach, we realized that the specialists were not what we were looking for. We needed to find someone who we could trust, but who also knew a lot about health. We immediately thought of Doctor Rosie O'Rabbit. As Sammy went to get Rosie, Kip suggested that Maggie might be able to help, as well. I agreed, and told Kip to go get her. It seemed like Nut E. had been in Awesommus' pouch forever by the time Rosie and Maggie finally showed up. When they got there, Maggie pulled Nut E.'s head out of the pouch.

"Oh, Nuthaniel," Maggie said lovingly. "I heard you stopped the dam, and Kip told me what you are trying to do. I'm very proud of you, but I think you're going about it the wrong way. The doctor is here with me and she's going to take a look at you."

Nut E. slowly climbed out of the possum's pouch, weak and soaked with sweat. Rosie looked concerned as she reached up, grabbed one of her ears, pulled it down and held it against Nut E.'s chest. She was listening to his heart.

"I'm afraid there is no quick way to lose weight and keep it off," Rosie said as she examined Nut E.

She grabbed his tongue and pulled it out of his mouth. "Oh this doesn't look good," she said. "You are severely dehydrated. If you're not careful, you're going to pickle your gizzard. These fad diets just don't work, but don't worry. I'm here to help you. First, we are going to have to change your eating habits, my friend, and that is going to take some time."

"I don't have time," Nut E. said. "I need to lose weight

fast. Thanks anyway, but I don't need your help."

Just then a skunk came running up to Nut E.
"Am I late?" he asked. The skunk quickly turned around and raised his tail. "This is called aromatherapy," he said, as he sprayed Nut E. directly in the face.

This caught Nut E. off guard. His eyes teared up and he began gagging as everyone else scattered.

"Now you will probably experience some slight nasal discomfort," the skunk explained. "But I'll bet you're not hungry."

Wiping the tears from his eyes, Nut E. slowly turned to Rosie and said, "Okay, where do we start?"

Hearing this Maggie smiled, hugged Nut E., and said, "First thing you need to do is take a shower." Then she pulled back, looked into his eyes and said, "I know you can do it."

"Well, if you're serious about this, you are going to have to listen to everything I say," Rosie said. "Go home, get some rest, drink plenty of water, and meet me at my office first thing tomorrow morning."

Sammy and I were relieved that Rosie had agreed to help Nut E. She really seemed to know what she was talking about, and that was going to make our job a lot easier. But I was still worried about how much time it was going to take because time was something we didn't have a lot of.

When we arrived at Rosie's office the next morning, it was very crowded. There were several patients, and at least two nurses helping Rosie care for them. It was very busy, but as I looked around, I was amazed to see how smoothly everything was running. The two nurses were rabbits like Rosie, and the three of them moved very quickly. We walked past the first nurse's station, where I saw Chainsaw the beaver sitting on an examination table. One of the nurses was looking down his throat with a lightning bug tied on the end of a stick, and when she put the stick in Chainsaw's mouth, the bug lit up.

"I think a piece of bark went down the wrong pipe," Chainsaw said in a scratchy voice.

We continued walking, and soon we reached the second station. This time, we found Dr. Rosie O' Rabbit talking to a groundhog. He was sitting on the table and holding an ice pack on his ear. The groundhog seemed very angry.

"I was just standing there, minding my own business!" he shouted. "When suddenly, from out of nowhere, someone threw a turnip at me. It hit me right in the side of the head."

Rosie slowly turned away from him and shook her head back and forth. "That's just my brother Danny. Oh Danny," she said, staring off into space, "when will you ever learn? It's all fun and games until someone loses an ear."

Further on, we saw the second nurse putting a neck brace on an old white mouse. He had a bandage wrapped around his chest, and a cast on his leg.

When we finally reached the last station, Rosie O'

Rabbit had hurried over to talk to Lewis the Turtle. He was shaking all over and talking very fast. "I think I'm shell shocked," he said. "Is there anyway I could get workman's comp? I really need a vacation."

When Nut E. saw Lewis, he reached up and patted him on the back. "I'm sorry about that little incident the other day." Nut E. said chuckling.

Lewis turned around, saw Nut E., and screamed. "Ahhh! It's him! He's the one I was telling you about! You've got to help me Doc! You've got to help me get this squirrel off my back!"

Nut E.'s eyes widened and he quickly turned around, trying to blend in with the rest of the crowd.

Lewis looked at him angrily and yelled. "You are banned from Turtle Crossing, Sir. Do you hear me? BANNED!"

Sammy and I looked at each other when Lewis said this. It was now very obvious that only way Nut E. Squirrel was going to get across that river was to jump across Tree Top Gap. Our job had just become much harder. Lewis continued to shout as we walked to the back of the office.

"You had better never show your face there again!" the turtle warned.

Nut E. pretended not to hear Lewis, but I could tell that he was very embarrassed. After Rosie finally calmed Lewis down, she followed us into her office and began setting up some sort of homemade scale, which she had made up of a string, two baskets, and some stones. The baskets were attached to each end of the string, which hung over a beam in the ceiling. One basket was filled with stones, and the other was empty.

"This is called a scale," Rosie began. "It was invented by my great grand dad, and what it does is measure your weight. This will show us how much progress you're making."

Then Rosie asked Nut E. to step up into the empty basket. When he did, it sank to the ground, and pulled the other basket, which was full of stones up into the air. To balance the scale, and to see exactly how much Nut E. weighed, Rosie began adding more stones, one by one, to the other basket. Eventually, Nut E. rose up into the air, and the two baskets hung side by side

"Mmmmm," Rosie said, counting the stones. "Okay, right now you weigh 11 stones. With your height and build, you should weigh about 7 stones. So that will be our goal. It is going to be a slow process. But like I said before, if you do what I say, and you don't give up, you'll be there before you know it."

I began to worry when Rosie said this. "Slow process," I said. "How long do you think it will take before Nut E. gets to his ideal weight?"

"Well, when losing weight, you don't want to go too fast now," Rosie warned.

"Why not?" I asked, confused.

"Here, let me show you what I mean."

Rosie tied a short piece of string to a separate beam just above her head. Then she tied the other end of the string to a little rock so that it hung down from the beam.

"Okay, Nut E.," she began. "Let's pretend that this rock is your weight. When it hangs straight down, that is your ideal weight position." Then she grabbed the rock and pulled it out to one side. "This is where your weight is right now. If you change your eating habits, and start eating healthy, you will lose weight slowly." As she said this, she slowly lowered the rock back to where it was and let it go. The rock just hung there straight up and down.

"As you can see, if you go slowly enough, when you reach your ideal weight, you will stay there, just like this rock. Now if you try to go too fast by using crash diets," she said as she pulled the rock back up to where she had held it before. "You'll lose a lot of weight, but you will gain it right back."

She released the rock. It swung down past the ideal weight position; and just as quickly as it fell, it swung back up. When it did, Rosie caught it in mid air.

"There's no sense in doing all that work, just to end up here right back where you started. Now like I said, it's going to take some time, but it will be worth it in the long run."

Nut E. had a smile on his face when she said this, but Sammy and I were a little concerned.

Seeing the worried look on my face, Sammy leaned over to me and whispered: "Don't worry, C.J. Even though Nut E. has a lot of work to do to get to his ideal weight, he doesn't have to be at his ideal weight just to get across the river."

I felt better as Sammy said this.

"Okay, Rosie, that sounds good," Nut E. said, stepping out of the basket. "So how do I change my eating habits?"

Rosie looked at Nut E., slowly smiled, and said, "Well, you're in luck. It just so happens that I'm giving a seminar on healthy eating in about an hour. You are all more than welcome to attend. This should clear up a lot of your questions about proper eating habits. But right now, let's focus on what has caused this problem in the first place. You see, what you need to understand is that there are literally hundreds of different reasons why animals are overweight. Everybody is different. For example, it could be because your parents passed down to you certain traits, like your brown eyes, bushy eyebrows, or maybe in this case, being overweight. Or, then again, maybe something traumatic happened to you when you were younger that caused you to feel unworthy of being healthy. Whatever the cause, you obviously developed some bad eating habits. That's when you began to form a picture of yourself in your brain as being fat. What we have to do now is to change that overweight picture that you have of yourself. You need to start visualizing what you would look like if you were thinner and healthier. When your mind can see yourself healthy, your body will begin to change. It's like my old brother Leptin used to say. 'If you point your mind in the right direction, your body will follow.'"

Nut E. thought for a moment, and said, "I am confused, how will this help me lose weight."

"Well, it's simple," Rosie said. "If you begin to see

yourself thinner and healthier, it will change your attitude towards food, and you won't be as hungry."

Nut E. looked up into the air and thought for a moment. "Oh, okay," he said smiling "I think I am beginning to understand."

"Good," Rosie replied. "Then let me show you what I want you to do."

Rosie took Nut E. out the back door of her office, and walked him over to the riverbank. Then she told him to look at his reflection in the water.

"What do you see?" Rosie asked.

"I see a big fat squirrel," Nut E. mumbled.

"Okay," Rosie said. "Now concentrate. Think about what you would look like if you were healthy."

"It's hard. All I see is fat," Nut E. said frustrated.

"Well, then you're going to have to practice. Every morning, I want you to look at your reflection in the water, and try to see yourself healthy. When you start changing the way you see yourself on the inside, your body will begin to change on the outside. So please Nut E., remember that it's not your fault. Just have hope, don't quit, and always remember that you are a good-hearted squirrel, and you deserve to be healthy."

As she said this, Nut E.'s face lit up, and you could see he felt much better. "It's not my fault," he said to himself.

This must have been the first time someone truly cared enough to find out who Nut E. really was, and taken the time to help him with his weight problem. Sammy and I were very glad that we had chosen Rosie to help us. We were feeling great, until the smile on Nut E's face began to fade away. His eyes took on a look of sadness as he slowly turned and walked away.

"Who am I kidding? Rosie, you don't understand. It *is* my fault," he said.

Nut E. walked upstream to a tree and sat down by himself, staring at the river. None of us knew what to think. We just stood there looking at each other until Rosie turned toward Maggie and asked: "Maggie, what's wrong with Nut E.?"

"I think you were right Rosie," Maggie said. "I'm pretty sure something traumatic did happen to him when he was younger, but I don't know what it was."

Rosie sighed. "This is going to be harder than I thought. Not only are we going to have to change the way he sees himself, but now were also going to have to figure out what is bothering him. You see, this could be what is keeping him from changing the mental image that he has of himself. If we don't find out what happened, no matter what I say, he will continue to use food to deal with this emotional problem. I don't know him well enough to help him deal with this issue. He needs a friend right now. And I think that friend is you, Maggie."

"I'll do what I can," Maggie said.

As Rosie turned around and went back into her office, Sammy and I spoke with Maggie about the challenges that faced Nut E. We realized it was all working out pretty well. Rosie was going to help the Mayor with his diet;

Maggie was going to help him with his emotional problem; and Sammy and I were going to teach him how to get across Tree Top Gap. Not wanting to waste any time, Maggie walked over towards Nut E., sat down next to him, and held his hand.

"I think something is bothering you, Nuthaniel," Maggie said. "Do you want to talk about it?"

Nut E. looked uncomfortable as she said this, and no matter how hard she tried, he continued to deny that he had a problem.

"I think you would feel much better if you would just talk to me about it," Maggie said. "Don't you understand, if you keep your problems bottled up inside of you, negative emotions will settle in your stomach leaving a hole that you can't fill with food. You have to fill it with love and understanding. I know it seems difficult, but all you really have to do is find the source of the problem— just like you did when the river was contaminated. Remember, everybody was sick and there were no fish eggs hatching. You marched right up to Section 1, found the source of the problem, and pulled that old paint can right out of the river. You saved us all."

"A lot of good it did," he said, staring out at the water. "There are still no fish eggs hatching?"

Maggie slowly reached up, grabbed his chin, and turned his face towards hers. She looked deep into his eyes. "Listen Nuthaniel, this is going to take time, so I am not going to pressure you. Whenever you are ready, you and I will deal with this problem together, but for right now, all I want to know is why it is so important for you to cross the river?"

Nut E. got real quiet, and he looked very sad. "My mother is over there," he said. "And I haven't seen her in a very long time. I heard that she is sick. She is over there all alone, and she needs me." Nut E. stopped as tears welled up in his eyes. "Don't you understand, Maggie? I have to find a way to get across that river, and I have to do it soon."

When I overheard Nut E. tell Maggie the reason he had to get across the river, it made me want to help him even more. No wonder he had hired the beavers to build the dam. It all began to make sense. We were so caught up in our own problems that we never took the time to ask ourselves what Nut E.'s reasons were. It was then that I made a promise to myself that I would not leave until Nut E. and his mother were once again reunited.

Food for Thought

aggie and Nut E. continued talking for a little while by the river. Even though Nut E. never actually told her what was bothering him, just talking to her seemed to make him feel better. And by the time we all made our way back into Rosie's office, Nut E. was back to his normal self. Rosie led us to a door that had the words *Children's Food Seminar* written on it. Inside, there must have been fifty little rabbits running around all over the place. They were screaming and yelling, climbing on chairs, and jumping off tables. They were everywhere.

"This is usually just a class I give to the children," Rosie said looking over at Nut E. "But under the

81

circumstances, I think it would do you a lot of good to hear it as well. I hope you don't mind sharing the room with the kids."

Nut E. quickly looked around the room. "Oh . . . well . . . Ah," he stammered. "I don't think this is a very good idea . . . I don't–"

"Look how cute they are," Maggie interrupted, smiling.

Nut E. looked at her, then back at the kids. I could tell that Nut E. didn't want to go into the room, but he didn't want to look bad in front of Maggie, either. So, he put a fake smile on his face and turned to Rosie.

"Why, no," he said. "I don't mind at all."

"Great," Rosie said, pointing towards the room. "Then, come on in and find a seat."

We all followed Rosie into the room. One of the little rabbits jumped off a tall cabinet and onto Nut E.'s back.

"Good gracious," the Mayor yelled. "They're attacking me."

Maggie laughed. "Oh Nuthaniel, they're just playing."

When Nut E. heard this, he tried to act like he was having fun. He bounced the little rabbit up and down a couple times, and let out a fake chuckle.

"Okay, there you go. All right son, the ride is over." Nut E. pulled the rabbit off his back, and patted him on the head. "There you go...be on your way now."

As Nut E. shooed the child away, something caught his eye. In the corner, a chubby little rabbit stood surrounded by two older rabbit's who were making fun of him.

"Look, Bobby," one of the older rabbits said. "Weedeater looks even fatter than he did yesterday." Suddenly, the older rabbit leaned down and rubbed little Weedeater's belly in a circle. "I wish I had a watermelon!" he yelled.

Everyone laughed, everyone except for the chubby little rabbit.

"Stop that!" Weedeater said, looking embarrassed.

Just then, the other older rabbit, Bobby, reached down, grabbed Weedeater's ankle and lifted it up into the air. As Weedeater hung there upside down, Bobby yelled, "Hey look, everybody, I found a lucky rabbit's foot."

The room exploded into laughter again. Little Weedeater looked humiliated.

"But Bobby," Weedeater said quietly. "That's my rabbit's foot."

Nut E. began to get angry. He immediately walked over towards the three little rabbits. When he reached them, he helped the chubby rabbit back onto his feet, and told the other two to sit down. Then, Nut E. put his arm around Weedeater and said, "Why don't you come sit over here by me young fella?"

Weedeater's face lit up as he followed Nut E. to their seats. When Rosie finally got all the children seated and quieted down, she began to speak.

"We have a very special surprise today children," Rosie said, smiling. "We have a celebrity in our class. Please join me in welcoming the squirrel who saved the river, the Honorable Nut E. Squirrel."

All the children clapped and cheered. At that moment, I felt proud just to be a part of the Mayor's team. It was almost like being famous. Nut E., who was used to all this, just shyly smiled and waved to the kids. Maggie clapped very loud, and smiled proudly.

It was obvious that she really liked Nut E. Just then, Weedeater looked up and said, "Thank you for helping me, Mr. Mayor. It is very nice to meet you."

Nut E. smiled as he shook the child's hand. "Please, son," he said. "Call me Nut E. That's what my friends call me."

"Well, in that case," the little rabbit replied. "You can call me fatso. That's what my friends call me."

Rosie looked at the kid and said, "Weedeater, leave the Mayor alone."

"Oh, he's fine," Nut E. said. "He's not bothering me."

I think Nut E. really liked Weedeater. I think in someway the child reminded Nut E. of himself when he was a kid.

Just then, one of the other children yelled out.: "Look, now Weedeater is not the fattest one in the room anymore."

Little Weedeater smiled proudly. Nut E. looked around angrily. But when all the children started to laugh, Nut E. put on another fake smile, and pretended the insult didn't bother him.

"All right, children," Rosie said, quieting the class. "That's enough. We have a lot of work to do today, so we should get started. Today, we are going to learn about all the different foods we eat. Now, there are many different food groups we can choose from when we are deciding what we should eat."

Rosie reached down and picked up a basket full of food that she had sitting on the desk in front of her.

"Now, in this basket," she said. "I have several different types of fruits, vegetables, grains, and nuts. The key is balance. Here, let me show you how this works." Rosie took one of the nuts out of the basket, and held it up for everyone to see. "For instance, let's say that all you ever ate was foods from the meat or nut group," she said, tossing the nut up into the air and catching it.

After she did this a couple of times, she looked at the kids once again. "Not very exciting, is it?"

One of the children sitting up front said, "No, it's actually kind of boring."

"You're right, it is boring," Rosie agreed. "And it's not very healthy for you either. But if I add food from some of the other groups, like fruits or vegetables, watch what happens."

Rosie reached into the basket and pulled out an apple and a carrot. She threw them up into the air, with the nut, and began juggling them in a big circle. The children cheered as they watched the food go round and round. I could tell by the way she juggled that she had done this many times before. It was amazing how she could hold the children's interest while at the same time educating them about healthy eating. Rosie, who was still juggling the food, continued to talk about the value of eating balanced meals and all the different food groups. As she did, I looked back and noticed that Nut E. was looking at the chubby little bunny sitting beside him.

When Weedeater looked up, Nut E. leaned over and whispered, "So, what do you think?" he asked.

Weedeater just shrugged. his shoulders and said

"I'm not sure. To tell you the truth, I'm kind of confused."

Nut E. smiled and said "Me too."

"I'm not sure how all this food group stuff is supposed to help me lose weight," Weedeater said. "But Dr. Rosie is really smart, and if she says it will work, then I guess it will."

"Well," Nut E. said, without hesitating, "everybody seems to think I need to lose some weight, but I'm not so sure. I really don't mind being fat."

"Are you kidding me?" Weedeater said in shock. "Why in the world would you not mind being fat? Being fat is no fun at all. I hate being fat! I can't run fast. I can't climb things very well. Everybody makes fun of me all the time. And Dr. Rosie says if I don't start eating healthier foods, and if I keep gaining weight, I could have some serious problems with my body when I get older. I want to learn everything I can about healthy eating. I don't want to end up old and fat and unable to do simple things that everyone else can do. You know things like . . ." Weedeater thought for a moment.

Nut E. looked very sad as he leaned over and whispered, "Things like crossing the river?"

"Yeah, things like crossing the river," the little bunny

repeated. "Besides, I'm tired of being teased about my weight."

Nut E. nodded. "Me too." he said.

I turned back around towards Rosie and heard her say: "So, you see, we need to eat little bit from all the food groups to maintain proper health."

"Dr. Rosie, the Mayor and I are a little confused," Weedeater yelled from the back of the room. "Will mixing up the food groups help us lose weight?"

"Well it's a start, Weedeater," Rosie answered. "But unfortunately, animals that are overweight like you and Mayor Nut E. will have to learn to eat less than you are eating now."

Nut E. looked confused.

"What do you mean, Rosie?" Nut E. asked.

"Well, Nut E.," she said. "You are going to have to start eating in moderation. For instance, if you normally eat three nuts for breakfast, try just eating two nuts. Eventually, your stomach will get used to the smaller portions, you'll be less hungry, and you'll begin to lose weight."

That is when a very skinny little rabbit stood up and asked, "Should I start eating less food, Dr. Rosie?"

Rosie got a very serious look on her face.

"No, sweetheart," she said. "When I was talking about eating less food, that is only for animals who are overweight. Being too thin is just as unhealthy as being too fat. Good health is all about being good to your body and listening to it. If you pay attention, your body will tell you exactly what it needs. Now in your case, you actually look a little thin. You may want to try eating a little more food."

We were all learning a lot about healthy eating that day, and I was sure that this was going to help Nut E. lose a lot of weight. I knew that if the Mayor did what Rosie was teaching him that Sammy and I would have him across that river in no time. I was feeling pretty good about Nut E.'s progress, but then I noticed Telly Vision sneaking in the back door, and crawling over towards the Mayor. He leaned over and whispered into Nut E.'s ear.

"Don't listen to that rabbit. You know you've just gotta have it. That grumble in your gut wants a sap covered nut."

Nut E. desperately tried to ignore him, but Telly just kept singing his little song over and over, until Nut E. couldn't take it anymore.

When Rosie finished speaking, she looked over at Nut E. and asked, "So, Mr. Mayor, did you learn anything today?"

When she looked at him, Rosie saw Nut E's face covered with sap. The Mayor was shoving the last bit of nut into his mouth.

"Nut E., why are you eating that?" she asked. "Are you that hungry?"

"Well, no. Actually, I'm kind of full," Nut E. replied. "But Telly made it sound so good, I just couldn't resist."

Rosie shook her head. "Nut E., you need to learn the difference between mouth hunger and stomach hunger.

What just happened to you was mouth hunger. Your stomach was full, but your taste buds couldn't resist the sap-covered nut. From now on, you need to eat only when you're stomach is hungry. And whatever you do, don't let T.V.'s commercials influence you into eating something you really don't want. You see, that sap is full of sugar, and if you eat too much of it, it will make you feel sick, and it really isn't very good for your body."

After she finished speaking, Rosie walked over to the Mayor, and put her arm around him. "Mr. Mayor," she said. "We still have a lot of work to do, but we had a very good day, and I think we got off to a great start."

"Well, I don't know Rosie," Nut E. said. "That was an awful lot of information. How am I supposed to remember everything you talked about?"

"Don't worry about it, Nut E. Just remember to balance your food groups, eat smaller portions, and if you have to have a snack, try eating a piece of fruit, or maybe a vegetable. They are much better for you than sap covered nuts."

Nut E. was a little hesitant. "Well, I'm pretty sure I can eat less, and balancing my food groups doesn't sound too bad. But Rosie," he said, protesting. "Snacking on only fruits and vegetables seems like an awful lot to ask."

When Rosie heard this, she frowned and said

"Well, I would think that eating healthier snacks from now on wouldn't be too difficult for the squirrel who saved the river." Rosie looked up at all the children. "What do you think kids? Do you think Mayor Nut E. can do it?"

All the little rabbits began cheering and yelling "yes." The children all jumped from their seats and quickly surrounded the flustered Nut E. Squirrel. One of the kids reached over and hugged Nut E.'s leg. She looked up at him, and in a very shy voice, she said: "You can do it, Mr. Mayor. I know you can." Then another child grabbed onto his other leg and held on tight.

Nut E. looked over at Rosie and said, "Okay, Rosie, I'll give it a try."

All the children cheered again. Rosie patted Nut E. on the back and leaned over to whisper in his ear: "Don't worry, Mr. Mayor, I'll help you."

Nut E. said goodbye to all the children, and he, Kip and Maggie began making their way home. Feeling kind of sluggish, Nut E. looked down and realized that the two baby rabbits were still clinging to his legs.

"Kip, take a note. Have these rabbits removed," Nut E. said.

Everybody laughed.

As Sammy and I were saying goodbye to Rosie, an excited Peety the Chipmunk came racing up, waving his arms around wildly as he spoke.

"I need supplies . . . I need supplies . . . I need honey. I need string . . . I need supplies."

Rosie just smiled as Peety rambled on.

"I'm gonna need 56 gallons of honey, and about 3 to 400 pieces of string. I haven't had time to figure out the exact amount, but that should get me off on the right foot . . . or the left foot. Actually, it really doesn't matter, because I won't be using my feet. I'm going to be flying. I'm building a flying machine. Have I told you that? Did I tell you I need some honey, and so . . . wait a minute . . . you wouldn't happen to have a scuba suit, would ya?"

Rosie and Peety walked off into the distance, leaving Sammy and I to talk about how well the project was going. I loved working with the Mayor. And Sammy loved being a part of such a glorious adventure.

Later that day, we had dinner with Nut E. and Kip. Nut E.'s eating habits had already begun to change, and he seemed more determined than ever. He ate a well-balanced dinner with plenty of fruits and vegetables, and he made an effort to eat less than he normally would have. Everything seemed to be going very well, until later that night.

We were all sitting around in Nut E.'s office talking about our plan to get Nut E. across the river. Sammy was explaining what we were going to do, and Kip was taking notes.

Nut E. leaned back in his chair, and patted his belly. "Okay, Kip, I think we have done enough work for one day. It's time for a snack. I need something sweet." The Mayor pointed to a huge pile of nuts in the corner. "Kip, I'm pretty sure that there is a sap covered nut buried in there somewhere," he said. Why don't you be a good little fellow and fish it out for me."

Kip looked at Nut E. with a worried look on his face.

"But Mr. Mayor," Kip said. "You promised Rosie you would eat only fruits and vegetables for snacks."

Nut E. smiled, slowly stood up, and waddled over to the big pile of nuts. "Don't worry about it, Kip. She will never know."

Nut E. then reached over and started digging through the nuts. It wasn't long before he found what he was looking for. As he grabbed the sap-covered nut, he uncovered the disappointed face of Dr. Rosie O'Rabbit, who had been hiding inside the pile. Nut E. looked stunned when he saw her.

"Uh . . . uh," Nut E. stammered, embarrassed. "How did this nut get in my hand? Kip, this isn't a carrot. I asked for a carrot. Don't you realize this will ruin my diet?"

Kip's looked nervously at Rosie O' Rabbit.

"You're right," Rosie said. "That *will* ruin your diet, but this wont."

Rosie took the sap-covered nut from Nut E.'s hand, and replaced it with a celery stalk. Nut E. reluctantly began chewing on the celery as Rosie climbed up out of the pile. She walked over to Sammy and me.

"Listen fellas," she whispered. "I can't be here all the time to make sure that the Mayor stays on his diet. I'm going to need your help. From now on, I want you to make sure that he only eats fruits and vegetables as snacks"

Sammy and I agreed to help. And as the days went on, Nut E. began to make progress. He stared into the river every morning, trying to see himself as a healthy squirrel. And with our help, he only ate fruits and vegetables as snacks. So when it was time for the Mayor to weigh himself again, we were all very excited.

"Nut E., you're down to ten stone. You have lost some weight. That is very good." Rosie said, as she finished measuring him on the scale.

Rosie seemed excited, but Nut E. wasn't. It was very clear that he still doubted himself.

"Rosie," Nut E. said, "I've been looking at my reflection every morning, but I am still having trouble seeing myself healthy. I know I have lost some weight, but all I can see is a big, fat, nut-craving loser. All I want to do is eat everything in sight."

"Well, that's normal when you are first starting out," Rosie explained. "But don't worry, as your body gets used to eating less food, the cravings will not be as strong. Hang in there Nut E.! Try to remember, you are not just changing the way you eat, you are changing the way you think. It's not going to happen overnight. It's going to take some time."

When Rosie said this, a sinking feeling filled my chest. I quickly turned towards Sammy and began to whisper.

"Sammy, time is the one thing we don't have. I hope we can get everything done before we need to leave for Butterfly Island."

Sammy nodded his head and thought for a moment. Then he looked at Nut E. and said "What do you think, Nut E? You've lost a little weight. Do you think you are ready for Tree Top Gap?"

"Sounds good to me," Nut E. said, relieved. "I've had about enough of this dieting stuff."

THE ADVENTURES OF NUT E. SQUIRREL

Rosie didn't say a word as we made our way towards the river. When we got there, Kip helped Nut E. slowly drag his overweight body up the tree, and before long they were standing on one of the branches that made up Tree Top Gap. Nut E. stared down nervously at the ground below. Trying to make Nut E. feel better, Sammy told Kip to find a long vine to use as a safety harness. Kip quickly found a vine, and tied one end of it to Nut E. Then he wrapped the other end of the vine around the branch three times and lowered it to the ground. Kip climbed down the tree and took hold of the vine. That way, if Nut E. fell from the limb, Kip could prevent Nut E. from falling into the water.

"Okay, here we are," Sammy said. "Just a quick little jump Nut E., and we will be sitting on the other side of this river before you know it."

Nut E. looked very worried as he took a deep breath, and slowly walked out to the edge of the limb. He looked down at the raging river beneath him, and his legs began to shake. Just then, the wind picked up, and the limb we were standing on began to sway back and forth. Nut E. quickly turned around and hurried back to where we were standing before.

"I don't know guys," he said. "Maybe this diet thing isn't such a bad idea. We need to give it some more time. Maybe we can come back after I've lost some more weight—"

"Don't worry about it, Nut E.," Sammy interrupted. "Everything is taken care of. All you have to do is take a running jump, spring off this limb, and land on the other side. There's nothing to worry about."

Nut E. didn't look very convinced.

"But what if I should fall?"

"That's what the safety vine is for," Sammy encouraged. "Kip won't let you fall."

Nut E. shook his head back and forth. "Ahh, I don't know, guys. I still think we're rushing things a bit."

Sammy thought for a moment. "I'll tell you what, Nut E. When you jump off the limb, C.J. and I will grab on to you and help fly you across."

Reluctantly, Nut E. agreed to make the jump. And on the count of three, we went. Nut E. began racing towards the end of the limb as fast as he could. Sammy and I each grabbed the fur on Nut E.'s shoulders and began flying along with him. When he reached the end of the branch, Nut E. sprang into the air, and Sammy and I flapped our wings as hard as we could. This worked perfectly, for about a second and a half. Then everything went horribly wrong. His huge body immediately plummeted towards the ground, the slack in the vine instantly tightened, and Sammy and I just hovered in the air, looking at each other blankly with only handfuls of Nut E.'s fur clenched in our fists.

The safety vine around the limb began to spin out of control. It reeled so fast that the limb was smoking and you could hear a high-pitched whistling sound coming from the vine. The vine was moving incredibly fast, and so was the determined little chipmunk who was desperately holding on to the other end of it. Kip was a blur of brown fur as he shot straight up into the air, spun around the limb three times before he was ripped back down to the ground below. Sammy and I heard a splat, and raced down towards the riverbed to see if everyone was all right. Nut E. and Kip were embedded in the mud along the riverbank. They were o.k., but our chances of leaving anytime soon seemed hopeless.

At that moment Rosie O'Rabbit came racing up beside Sammy and I. We were all staring at the Mayor and his deputy lying face down in the mud. Kip stood up and began wiping mud off his fur. We were all a little sad, but not nearly as sad as Nut E. Squirrel, who just sat there in the mud. Rosie walked over to Nut E. and crouched down right in front of him. She lifted his head, wiped the mud out of his eyes, and spoke very softly.

"I know you're tired. I know you're scared. I know you feel like you can't do this. Your whole world is changing, and you have nothing to hold onto. But you are much stronger than you think you are. You are just going to have to reach down deep inside of yourself and find the courage to be strong."

When Rosie finished speaking, the sad look on Nut E.'s face began to fade into a smile. I could tell Nut E. was beginning to feel much better as Rosie slowly lifted him back onto his feet. As Nut E. began brushing himself off, Rosie put her arm around him and spoke once again.

"You've done good work, Nut E., and I'm proud of you," Rosie said. "There is still a lot more work to be done, but it's good work. And when you complete this journey, your entire life will be better. You will be better. Now, go home, get some rest, and we will start fresh tomorrow morning."

Nut E. nodded his head, turned, and began walking away. Mud still hung from his overweight body, as the humbled Nut E. Squirrel hobbled his way back home.

We all stood there in silence for a few minutes. We felt the tremendous pain and sorrow that our friend Nut E. was feeling, and we knew that something more must be done. His body weight was dragging him down, and that was going to have to change, and change fast!

"Boys, I need you to do me another favor," Rosie said seriously. "I can only do so much for Nut E. I can teach him about eating properly balanced meals, and eating less, but he needs to start moving his body more. He needs to exercise. This is where you guys come in. We need to get someone that can help him exercise, and there's only one squirrel that can do it."

Rosie looked directly at Kip. The Deputy Mayor appeared somewhat confused at first, but then his eyes popped wide open.

"Rosie, do you mean that you want us to go get . . ." Kip trailed off, unable to speak.

"Yes, Kip," Rosie said. "We need the best . . . so go get him!"

Confused, I finally blurted, "What is going on here?"

Kip looked at me very seriously, took a deep breath, than exhaled slowly. "Champion," he finally said.

Then he was quiet. He looked as if just saying the name had frightened him.

Champion? Where have I heard that name before? I thought to myself. Then it hit me. That was the name of the amazing squirrel that had saved Sammy and I from the spider's web just a few days before.

"They say Champion can do anything," Kip said. "But nobody really knows for sure because he hasn't come down from his tree for a long time."

"Why not?" I asked.

"Well, from what I hear," Kip began. "He used to come down all the time. He used to love to teach the children about health and exercise. But everything changed the day he decided to enter the Squirrel Olympics. At first, everyone was thrilled. But when Champion won every single event, tempers began to rise. No one could believe that he was actually that good. They accused him of cheating, called him a freak, and told him to go away. I think they were just afraid of him but all he felt was their hatred. After that, he vowed no one would ever see him again. Then he stood up in front of everyone, said 'I'm finished here,' and climbed back up to the very top branch of the Tree of Life . . . No one has seen him since."

Kip began pacing back and forth. "Now, I have never met Champion Squirrel. I have only heard about him in whispers late at night when no one else was listening, and I have to be honest with you, it scares me to death that this is the squirrel that Rosie O'Rabbit wants us to go find." Kip shook his head. "This is crazy. We don't even know if he's still alive!"

Just then, from behind me, I heard the excited voice of Samson J. Caterpillar. "He's alive," Sammy said confidently. "And we know exactly where he's at. C.J. and I saw him a couple of days ago."

"You did?" Kip asked.

"Sure," Sammy said. "And we can take you right to him."

Kip was reluctant at first, but Sammy and I finally talked him in to going. The Deputy Mayor looked worried as he began climbing the Tree Of Life, but Sammy and I assured him that everything was going to be fine. We hovered next to him as he climbed higher and higher up the Tree. The sun was beginning to set, but we were making good time. Soon, we all noticed a buzzing noise coming from up above. As we continued climbing, the buzzing noise seemed to surround us, and Kip looked more frightened than ever.

"Stay here, Kip," Sammy said looking up towards the top of the Tree.

Sammy flew up, and I quickly followed after him. We flew as high up the tree as we could before we finally had to stop. The buzzing sound grew so loud that it was hurting our ears. I wanted to turn back and motion to Sammy for us to go back down, but Sammy just shook his head and pointed up the tree. I looked up and saw what he was pointing at. It was the hole Peety the Chipmunk lived in; that was where the noise was coming from. We held our hands over our ears and struggled against the noise as we made our way up to Peety's home.

"Peety, are you alright?" I yelled.

Peety's old gray head popped up out of the hole. His excited eyes kept blinking, and his head kept spinning around inside the doorway of his home. Peety began yelling at the top of his voice. I had my hands over my ears because the buzzing noise was so loud that it was tough to hear anything else, but I managed to make out what that crazy old chipmunk was yelling.

"Hey!" Peety yelled. "Would you guys keep it down out there. I am working on something in here that will change the course of Chipmunk history. I can't even hear myself think with all that racket you two butterflies are making. Now, keep it down please. I'm working."

Kip scurried up and yelled over the tremendous buzzing noise: "What is going on?" Sammy pointed towards Peety's hole.

"Oh boy, what is cousin Peety up to now?" Kip asked, shaking his head.

Sammy smiled, went over to the hole, and looked inside. Kip and I looked inside, as well. We would never have guessed what we were about to witness. Peety had a hundred pieces of string tied to his body, and each piece of string was attached to a bee. The bees swarmed above Peety's head, and his entire body was covered with honey.

I couldn't believe what I was seeing. Sammy started

laughing, and Kip just shook his head and said

"Do you see why our family doesn't talk about him much?"

Peety just looked over at us and smiled.

"Well, I'm glad you're all here," Peety said. "You're just in time to witness the launching of my new flying machine. No longer will chipmunks be forced to climb on trees or walk on the ground. Today, we take to the air. Today we will go where only the birds have gone before, because today we take to the air."

Peety stopped, shook his head back and forth, and said

"Crimeney Sakes, did I say that already? Oh well, it doesn't matter, for today we take to the air. And as acting Owl, I will finally be able to soar above my domain to make sure everyone is safe."

Peety grabbed onto all the strings he could and shook them. "Let's go bees. We have a date with destiny."

When Peety shook the strings, the bees began to grow angry. We all dove out of the way as the bees drug Peety up out of the hole and into the sky. Peety looked down at the ground below, and he became more excited than I had ever seen him before. He began moving around wildly.

"That's it! I did it! This is a monumental day in the history of the meadow. The eagles are landing in Houston."

Peety was happily rambling on, but what he didn't realize was that every time he moved, he pulled a string, which pulled another bee out of the sky. As Peety continued squirming in the air, and yelling at the top of his voice, more and more bees were becoming angry. Finally, some of them began diving down and stinging him. At first, Peety was too excited to notice.

"That's one small step for chipmunks. One giant leap for . . . OUCH! Woah! Hey, I'm hit! OUCH! Hey, I'm hit again! They seem to have me surrounded . . . OUCH! I seem to have lost the feeling in the entire left side of my body. Crimeney Sakes, somebody help me! No, wait! Save yourself! Don't let me fool you into believing you can still save me. I'm delirious. I don't know what I'm saying...Don't worry. I'll be all right. They have got to land eventually...Who am I kidding? I'm doomed!"

Peety continued rambling as the bees carried him off into the sunset. We all stared out at Peety until we couldn't see or hear him any longer. Kip looked embarrassed as he looked out into the setting sun.

"Well this is definitely a low point for my family," Kip said.

He stood there still staring out into the darkening sky for a few more seconds. Then he just shrugged his shoulders and started climbing the Tree once again.

As the sun set behind us, I began to feel cold. Winter was letting us know that it was out there somewhere waiting for us. Waiting to strike! The chilly night air began to feel thick, making it difficult for us to breathe. As Kip climbed from one branch to the other, Sammy and I flew between them. The branches were like a maze. Kip was tired and scared, but bravely continued to climb. Sammy and I were squeezing in and out of the limbs one after another. I flapped my wings very slowly, trying to maneuver my body around the jagged branches. Sammy and I continued climbing and flew as carefully as we could, until, at last, we neared the home of Champion Squirrel. Our dangerous climb had come to an end, but something in the back of my mind told me to be careful, for the real danger might be just up ahead.

Playing to Win

Crickets chirped in the distance with the coming of night as we moved closer to Champion's home. My heart pounded with each twig that snapped under Kip's feet. Kip stopped, and as he cautiously looked around, he whispered, "Champion doesn't like visitors. Maybe we should just go back and get someone else to help us. I have a bad feeling about this."

I didn't want to go any further, either, but we were running out of time. I knew that the only one that could help us now was the mysterious squirrel that lived at the top of the Tree, the one they called Champion. Realizing Kip was scared, Sammy told him that he didn't have to go any further, and that we would go up and talk to Champion without him.

"Yeah, that's a good idea," he said, nodding frantically. "You guys go on without me. I'll stay back here and wait for you."

Just then, we heard the loud croak of a bullfrog off in the distance. Kip's eyes darted back and forth. "On second thought," he said. "Maybe I should go with you fellows. You may need me to protect you."

As we neared the top, the branches got smaller. Kip was having a hard time keeping his balance as the branches bent under his weight. "I can't believe a squirrel of Champion's size can walk on these branches," Kip whispered, as he struggled to hang on to the swaying limbs. "He must have amazing strength and balance."

"That's why we need to find him," Sammy said. "If anyone can get Nut E. into shape, he can."

Kip shook his head back and forth. "I still think this is a bad idea."

"Stop worrying Kip," Sammy said. "Everything is going to be just fine."

Suddenly, something snapped under Kip's feet. His ankles were immediately pulled together, and his legs were ripped out from under him. He was flipped upside down, and his body was hoisted up into the air. He had been caught in some sort of homemade snare trap that must have been set by Champion. As Kip dangled there by his feet swaying back and forth, he said, "I told you this idea was bad."

Just then, we heard a voice off in the distance. "Why have you come here?"

Sammy and I quickly turned around, and found ourselves looking at Champion. He stood way out at the end of a tree limb, so far that it appeared he was standing in midair. The full moon behind him cast a shadow over his entire body. His muscular form stood outlined in the darkness. He was doing some sort of martial arts exercise. He moved very slowly, but very precise, and by watching him, I could tell that he had been doing these exercises for a very long time. It was amazing. He had his back to us, and without looking, he knew exactly where we were and what we were doing. My heart felt like it was going to beat right out of my chest as I stood watching him dance on the wind. I wanted to fly away, but I knew I couldn't. So I took a deep breath, cleared my throat, and tried to speak in a calm voice.

"Excuse me, sir," I said in a scared, crackling voice. "My name is C.J., and this is my friend Sammy. We were the ones that you saved from the spider's web."

"I know who you are," he said, still not looking at us. "Why have you come here?"

Still in awe, I blurted out the first thing that popped into my head. "That was unbelievable what you did to that spider. I have never in my life seen anyone move the way you did. It was great!"

When Champion heard this, he stopped moving and slowly turned around to face us. I was surprised to see that he looked very angry.

"Great!" he said, as he slowly walked towards us. "Maybe you should tell that to the spider. He didn't eat that night, and he had to spend hours repairing the damage we did to his web."

I was confused.

"Well, if that's the way you feel, then why did you save us in the first place?"

"Because you both have children on the way, and eventually, they are going to need you." Champion said.

Then he wiped the sweat off his forehead with a leaf towel and threw it at me. I caught it as he turned around and walked over to a nearby tree limb, where a gourd hung by a small string. Champion took the gourd down and looked back at me.

"You still haven't answered my question," he said angrily. "Why have you come here?"

Champion pulled the lid off the gourd. It was full of water. Champion slowly lifted it to his mouth and began drinking. I looked at Sammy and he gave me a nod. I looked back at Champion and said

"Aaahh . . . we just wanted to thank you for saving us, that's all."

Champion lowered the gourd and stared at me for a long moment. He looked over at Sammy, then at Kip, who still hung upside down. He slowly took another drink, and hung the gourd back up in the tree. He turned around, and began to walk away.

"That is not why you came here," he said, as he reached up to a nearby limb and began doing pull-ups.

I looked at Sammy again for support, but he nodded toward Champion, as if to say, 'Just ask him.' So I mustered up my strength.

"Ahhh . . . we came to ask for your help," I said, fearing his response.

Champion stopped his pull-ups. "You need my help? Again?" he said with impatience.

"Well, actually, it's not for us," I replied quickly. "It's for a friend of ours. He needs to lose weight and get into shape. We were hoping you could help him."

"I don't train other animals anymore," he said, as he turned around and began to walk away. "I'm sure you can show yourselves out."

Desperately, I yelled, "Listen, Champion, all we are asking is—"

Champion whirled around and shot me another angry stare. "Why does everyone keep calling me that?"

I looked at him confused. "Because you won the Squirrel Olympics. You won every event. You're a champion."

This time, Champion was the one that looked confused. "Do you think that winning first place in some stupid sporting event makes someone a champion?"

Not knowing how to respond to his question, I just shrugged my shoulders and nodded my head "yes".

"Come here," Champion said, as he walked to the edge of the tree branch. "I want to show you something."

Sammy and I flew over beside him.

"Do you see that ant down there?" he asked, pointing towards the ground.

The bright moon lit up the meadow, and when I looked down, I could see an ant on the side of a small hill. He was all alone, but working very hard.

"That ant's home has been flooding for the past 6 days," Champion said. "So, not only has he spent the entire week working all day to gather food for his family, but he has spent every night building them a new home on higher ground. That ant has worked unselfishly day and night making sure his family has food and a dry place to sleep. *He* is the champion, not me."

Sammy slowly turned and looked at Champion. He spoke for the first time since we had arrived. "Well maybe part of being a champion is helping others when they ask for it."

Champion looked at Sammy and thought for a moment. Then he slowly smiled and asked, "Who is this friend you're asking me to help?"

It was Kip's turn to speak next. Still hanging upside down, he smiled proudly and said, "The honorable Mayor Nut E. Squirrel."

Champion's smile faded to anger. "Then my answer is NO!"

"No? What do you mean no?" Kip asked.

"Your friend is the reason that ant had to leave his home," Champion said, pointing again towards the ground.

"But you don't understand!" Kip shouted. "He stopped the dam. He—"

"All politicians are the same," Champion continued.

"They live off the sweat of the poor and get fat off bribes from the rich. How dare you come here and ask me to help someone like that."

Champion reached down and picked up his staff that was leaning against the trunk of the tree. He quickly walked towards Kip.

Kip's eyes widened and he gulped. "Uh, fellows," Kip said in a worried voice. "There's an angry squirrel with a stick coming at me."

I held my breath as Champion walked up to Kip, and stopped right in front of him. My worry turned to relief when he reached up, swung his staff, and cut the vine that held Kip up. The Deputy Mayor fell like a rock, landing on the limb below. Sammy and I rushed over to help him up.

"You've wasted your time," Champion said, and put down his staff. "Now take your friends and go home. I'm finished here."

Champion turned and began to walk away. Kip angrily stood up and brushed himself off.

"You're right," Kip yelled. "We did waste our time coming here, because you're no champion. You're a coward."

I couldn't believe what I had just heard. I looked over at Sammy, whose eyes were as wide as mine. I looked back at Champion, surprised to see that he was still just walking away.

"Let me tell you something about Mayor Nut E.," Kip said. "He's a better squirrel than you will ever be in your entire life."

My heart skipped a beat when Champion stopped walking. I thought he was going to come back and attack Kip, but he didn't. He just stood there with his back to us and listened as Kip proceeded to tell Champion all about the wonderful things Nut E. had done as Mayor. He told Champion about how Nut E. had personally carried food to the poor during the winter. He told him how he had donated his time helping the elderly. And he told him about how Nut E. had stopped the dam, even though he desperately needed to get across the river to see his ailing mother. The fact that Champion never turned around seemed to make Kip angrier than ever. When Champion simply walked away into the darkness, Kip began yelling even louder. "Mayor Nut E. Squirrel is the greatest squirrel I have ever known. And if you refuse to help him, then I feel sorry for you. You can just hide up here in your little tree house the rest of your life for all I care."

But Champion was gone.

We stood there in silence for a while. Then I flew over and put my arm around the tired little chipmunk. "Don't worry about it, Kip. We made a promise to Nut E., and we are going to keep it. We will get him across that river, even if we have to train him ourselves."

Kip smiled. As we made our way back down the tree, Sammy told him jokes until he was actually laughing again. When we got half way down the tree, we heard whimpering sounds coming from Peety the Chipmunk's home. We quickly flew down and looked inside. We saw Peety lying back in a chair with bee stings all over his body. He was gently smearing mud on them, and groaning in pain as he talked to himself.

"My trajectory was all wrong. What was I thinking? Those bees were savages. They were not disciplined at all. I need military bees. That's it. I will...I will find military bees and train them properly . . . I am a genius . . . I can . . ."

Kip climbed down beside us. "You're wasting your time Peety," Kip said. "Everybody knows that chipmunks can't fly. Why don't you just give it up?"

Peety looked at him, somewhat confused. "You're right Kip. Chipmunks can't fly. What was I thinking? I should just quit . . . I should just . . ."

"No, Peety," Sammy said. "You shouldn't quit."

Peety thought for a moment and said

"You're right. I shouldn't quit," Peety agreed. "...Huh, Quit! What was I thinking! I can't quit! I need to find a way to fly . . . I need to build some sort of flying machine, but hmmm . . . how can I fly?"

"Well, I don't know if it will help, Peety," I said. "But a very good friend of mine once told me the secret to flying,"

Peety's eyes widened. "He did? What did he say? What did he say?"

"He said if you cannot fly, your wings are too wide."

Peety quickly shook his head back and forth. "Crimeney Sakes! I don't have wings. That is the most ridiculous thing I have ever heard. I can't . . . Hey, that's it . . . WINGS! I will build wings. What a great idea. I'm a genius."

Forgetting his pain, Peety jumped up and grabbed a pencil and paper. He began pacing back and forth. "Let's see, I'm going to need some feathers, and some sort of glue. Let me see. . . two wings top and bottom . . . the total area divided by seven . . . carry the one."

As Peety disappeared back into his house, we continued down the tree. Nobody spoke, and I believe we were all thinking the same thing. Without Champion's help, we had to train Nut E. ourselves. And between the three of us, we knew exactly nothing about training. But Sammy had just told Peety not to quit, and we were not going to quit either. So the next morning, we set out to do the impossible

The sun began to rise as Nut E., Kip, Sammy and I all met beside the river. Nut E. looked very determined, and we were not about to let him down.

"I think we should start with some stretching exercises," Sammy said, as he looked over at me and shrugged his shoulders.

"Yeah, that sounds like a good idea," I said, shrugging back at him. "How about some deep-knee bends?"

We all started stretching out our arms and crouching up and down. Nut E. was smiling for the first two crouches, but on the third he went down and stayed down. He tried to push himself back up, but it was no use. He groaned and slowly toppled over on the ground. He laid there curled up in a ball gasping for air.

"It's no use," he said panting. "This is just too hard. I can't do it."

"That's because you're not doing it properly," a voice said from up above.

I quickly turned and looked up into the trees. It was Champion. He stood on a limb with his arms folded across his chest. He was leaning up against the trunk of the tree looking down at us.

As Nut E. looked up into Champion's eyes, he got a strange look on his face. "You look familiar to me, sir. Have we met somewhere before?"

"That's Champion Squirrel," I said, smiling. "I think he's going to help us."

"Champion Squirrel," Nut E. whispered. "I didn't think you were still around."

Champion stood there a moment, and then jumped down on the ground. As he walked up to Nut E., the Mayor pulled himself to his feet.

"I heard you stopped the dam," Champion said, ignoring Nut E.

Nut E. nodded. "Yes, I did," he said. "I realized that I was hurting a lot of other animals, so I told the beavers to stop building."

Champion stood there a moment, then finally said, "Let's get one thing straight. I don't like politicians. And I'm not fully convinced that you are the squirrel that everyone says you are. But your friends here seem to think you're worth the effort."

"He's a great squirrel," Kip said nervously.

Champion didn't look at Kip. He just kept staring at Nut E. Then he slowly nodded his head.

"If I agree to help you, are you going to do whatever I ask you to do, without question?"

Nut E. nodded again. "I need to get across that river."

When I realized that Champion was going to help us, I began to feel really good about the success of our mission. This was going to make our job a lot easier. Everything was going perfectly. All we needed to do was get Nut E. across that river, and now I was confident that we had found the right squirrel to help us. Just then, we heard a loud squawking noise coming from a branch up above us. When I looked up to see what was going on, I saw an angry bird dragging Peety the Chipmunk behind him. Peety was hanging on to one of the bird's tail feathers. He was leaning back with his feet out in front of him trying to pull a feather out of the bird's tail. As Peety skied behind the angry bird, he was yelling very loudly.

"I just need one feather," he screamed. "I know it hurts, but we all have to give. If I am going to fly over my domain as the acting Owl, then I need wings my friend, and those wings need feathers."

We all laughed as the bird pulled Peety out of sight.

"Okay Nut E.," Champion said, getting down to business. "There are three things that we are going to focus on in your training: stretching, resistance exercise, and cardiovascular work.

So let's not waste any more time. Lesson number one is stretching."

Nut E. slowly stretched out his arms, yawned and said, "Ahhhh . . . yeah, I could use a good stretch." The Mayor then scratched his belly. "That's the ticket. This exercise stuff is easier than I thought it would be."

Champion just smiled. "That's not quite what I was talking about. Actually, we haven't even started yet. Stretching is just a warm up for the real exercise. You don't want to pull a muscle. You need to stretch slow and steady before you start."

Champion began to teach Nut E. how to properly stretch. First, he bent down and touched his toes, which stretched his leg muscles. Then, he sat down on the ground, leaned forward, and touched his toes again, which stretched his legs even more. Champion continued to do stretching exercises until every muscle in his body was warmed up and ready to go.

"Stretching will make you very flexible, Nut E.," Champion explained. "And flexibility is strength. So why don't you give it a try."

Nut E. tried to stretch, but it was obvious that his heart wasn't in it. With every minute that passed, the other side of the river seemed further and further away. The exercise portion of Nut E.'s training wasn't going much better than his diet.

"Kip, this exercise stuff is making me hungry," Nut E. said. "I need a snack. Go get me a sap covered nut."

"Mr. Mayor, how can you be hungry?" Kip asked.

"We just ate breakfast an hour ago. Besides, you promised Rosie you were going to eat fruits and vegetables as snacks."

Nut E. became angry.   "Kip, don't argue with me. I've been working hard here. Just get me the nut."

Kip reluctantly handed him a sap-covered nut. Nut E. took the snack, and licked his lips. "Come to papa," he said, smiling.

As Nut E. lifted the nut to his mouth, I thought about the promise we made to Rosie, and I knew that I had to stop him. Just as I was about to fly over and take it from him, Sammy whizzed by me in an orange and black blur and replaced the nut in the Mayor's hand with a berry. When Nut E. bit down on what he thought was a nut, juice from the berry splattered everywhere. Nut E. looked around confused, but Sammy was nowhere in sight.

"Boy, he's good," I muttered.

Disgruntled, Nut E shoved the rest of the berry in his mouth.

"Kip, take a note. We need to put a bell on that butterfly, " the Mayor said, as he slowly walked back towards Champion.

"Wow, am I glad you guys are here," Kip whispered to me. "There's no way the Mayor could do this without your help."

I smiled proudly, glad that we had made the decision to stay.

"All right, Nut E.," Champion said. "It's time for lesson number two: resistance training."

"What's resistance training?" Nut E. asked.

"Well, Nut E., it's stuff like push-ups, sit-ups, and pull-ups. These kinds of exercises help to build muscles."

Nut E. quickly interrupted him and shouted, "But I'm not interested in building muscles! I just want to lose weight!"

"You will lose weight," Champion assured. "You see, as your muscles get bigger, they will cause you to burn more fat, and the weight will disappear."

After Champion said this, the training began. First, they tried doing push-ups. However, when Nut E. lowered his body down, he could not push himself back up.

"Kip, I need some assistance," Nut E. said with his face buried in the dirt. "This exercise stuff is harder than I thought."

Kip helped Nut E. up, and after a short rest, Nut E. tried pull-ups. He couldn't even do one.

"This is a waste of time," Nut E. complained. "I don't see how all of this monkey business will help me get across the river."

Champion walked over to Nut E., put his hand on his shoulder, and said, "I know it's hard work Nut E., and right now it's tough to see how this is all going to turn out. But I promise you, if you do what I tell you, it will become easier, and each day you will make progress."

Champion seemed to be starting to like Nut E. Squirrel. As the day went on, Champion introduced Nut E. to one exercise after another. And with each failed attempt, Nut E. became more and more discouraged.

119

Sensing Nut E.'s disappointment, Champion said, "Maybe it's time for a break. Why don't we play a game? It's called Tail Toss."

"Sounds good to me," Nut E. said. "I could use a break."

Champion grabbed a nut, cupped it in his tail, and flung it at Nut E. The Mayor caught the nut in his tail, and flung it back to Champion. For the first time that day, Nut E. finally enjoyed himself. The two continued throwing the nut back and forth harder and harder. They jumped over bushes, and ran through the woods trying to make each and every catch. When I saw Nut E. sweating, I realized that Tail Toss was not just a game, it was also an exercise. Nut E. was enjoying himself so much that he didn't even realize how hard we was working. After the game ended, Nut E. was breathing very hard.

"My heart is racing, and I'm worn out. What a fun game," Nut E. said, panting.

Champion just smiled and said

"Congratulations, Nut E. You just learned lesson number three: the value of cardiovascular exercise."

"Cardio what?" Nut E. asked confused.

"All that word means is that you are building the most important muscle in your entire body, your heart."

"Huh" Nut E. said. "I guess exercise can be fun too."

"You're right, Nut E. There are all kinds of fun little exercises we can do to help you lose weight. In fact, some of the best ways to exercise is to run around, jump, walk, or even play tag. Any movement of your body is healthier than sitting around doing nothing."

In the hours that followed, Champion showed Nut E. many different types of cardiovascular exercises, like jumping rope. Nut E. was really enjoying himself as he jumped up and down time and time again. But his excitement faded when he got tangled in the rope. The Mayor lost his balance, and dropped like a rock. Champion picked up the jump rope, and helped the frustrated Nut E. Squirrel back up onto his feet.

"This is ridiculous," Nut E. shouted. "I can't do any of these exercises."

Champion just patted him on the back. "Don't worry, Nut E. You will learn. Just give it time." Then Champion handed Nut E. a nutshell full of water, and said "Here, drink this. It will make you feel better."

Nut E. stared at the water with a disappointed look on his face.

"I would rather have some saparilla," he said. "It tastes better."

"What is saparilla?" Champion asked.

Nut E. smiled. "Saparilla is a delicious blend of sap and water. It tastes so sweet it makes your lips pucker." He said obviously repeating what he had heard from Telly Vision.

"When you are exercising, you should only drink water," Champion said. "Your body is tired right now, and you need to give it what it wants. And it wants water. Water will help your muscles work properly and keep you from getting tired so fast."

Nut E. drank the water. Then after a brief rest, Champion said it was time to start exercising again.

"I'm tired," Nut E. sighed. "I don't want to exercise any more today. Why don't we go do something else?"

Champion thought for a moment. "That's a good idea," he said. "Why don't we all go swimming?"

Nut E. looked nervous. "Do you mean . . . in the river? That's crazy. The current is much too strong."

Champion shook his head. "Of course we are not going to swim in the river. We can go to Tadpole Pond."

Nut E.'s eyes lit up. "Ooh yeah," he said. "That sounds like fun. I haven't swum since I was a kid."

As we made our way to the small pond on the other side of Tree Ville, I was surprised to see that Champion was ending that first day so early, but as I watched Nut E. go round and round in the water, I realized why Champion had brought us here. Swimming, like Tail Toss, was not only fun, but also a great exercise. After swimming for several hours, Nut E. was worn out. He slowly drug his tired body from the water, looking like a drowned rat. His soaked fur clung to his body, showing years of neglect and overeating. For the first time, I could see exactly how fat the Mayor really was. And I began to worry. We were running out of time, and we still had a long way to go.

Just then, Maggie emerged from the woods with a sympathetic look on her face.

"Oh Nuthaniel," she said. "Are you okay? You look very tired."

Seeing her, Nut E. frantically tried to hide his body by fluffing up his fur.

"Oh . . . ah . . . hi, Maggie," he said, embarrassed. "No, I . . . I'm fine. It really wasn't as bad as I thought. I'm really looking forward to getting an early start tomorrow."

Nut E. was obviously trying to impress Maggie. And seeing them together reminded me of Cat. I missed her a lot, even though it had only been a few days.

Maggie sat down beside Nut E. holding hands as they stared out over the water.

"Nuthaniel," Maggie said. "I think you and I should talk about what has been bothering you. Rosie thinks there is something from your past that you are keeping locked up inside. She says that if you talk about it with someone else, it will make you feel better."

Nut E. quickly began searching around. Soon, he found what he was looking for. He grabbed an acorn off the ground, and popped it into his mouth.

"No, no . . . nothing is really bothering me," he said, as he took a bite out of the nut. "It's just this whole river crossing thing. It's got me all tied up in knots."

Nut E. chewed very quickly, seeming nervous. Maggie eyed him curiously. "Well, Rosie seems to think that you are hiding something inside, and that it's causing you to eat too much food."

"That is ridiculous," Nut E. said, chomping down on the nut again.

Maggie reached over and gently grabbed Nut E.'s chin,

turning his head and looking deeply into his eyes. "Nuthaniel, it's okay," she said lovingly. "Just tell me what happened."

Nut E. tried to look away, but Maggie would not let him. "Please Nuthaniel, talk to me."

Nut E. thought for a moment, then slowly lowered his head. "There was an accident," he sighed. "My family had just moved here, and my little brother Tommy accidentally fell into the river and got washed downstream. He drowned at Danger Rapids. I wasn't there at the time, but my Mom was really upset."

Maggie looked at Nut E., stunned. "Oh Nuthaniel," she gasped, and covered her mouth with her hands. "That is horrible."

Rosie had been right all along. And though I felt uncomfortable listening to Nut E talk about his personal life, Sammy and I were in charge of his health and needed to know what was bothering him.

Nut E. composed himself and continued to speak. "It was pretty bad, but you know . . . these things happen. I've gotten over it, and moved on with my life." Nut E. began devouring the rest of the nut. "I don't think that is what causes me to overeat," he said, as little pieces of the nut sprayed out both sides of his mouth.

At that moment, Nut E. stood up.

"Ya know, Maggie, I really don't have the time to talk about this right now. I'm very tired, and I have a long day tomorrow. I really should go home and get some rest."

"But Nuthaniel," she said. "We need to talk about this."

Nut E. pretended like he didn't hear her, and walked off into the woods.

Sammy and I flew down beside Maggie. "He's in a lot of pain," she said with a concerned look on her face. "And until he admits it, there is really nothing we can do to help him."

"Don't worry, Maggie, Sammy said. "Nut E. has a lot of friends who are watching out for him right now. He will be o.k."

"I hope you're right," she said, and walked away.

As time passed, things started to improve. Nut E. ate only fruits and vegetables as snacks; and with Champion's help, he got stronger and better at all the exercises. He lost more weight, and got down to nine stones on Rosie's scale. But it was going much slower than we had planned. Even though Nut E. looked at his reflection every morning, he still could not imagine himself healthy, and it slowed him down. I got more and more worried as the days turned into weeks, and the temperature dropped. Sammy kept reminding me that we needed to leave before the snow, and I kept reminding him how important it was for us to stay and help Nut E. It was a tough time for Sammy and I, but it was about to get a lot tougher.

Chasing a Champion

On a particularly cold morning, Champion announced that he had a surprise for Nut E. He took Nut E. up into the trees and told him that they were going to run the Gauntlet. The Gauntlet was an obstacle course in the tree branches that had been built for the Squirrel Olympics. It was a series of climbs, jumps, turns, twists, and falls that would test Nut E.'s abilities. Champion told Nut E. that when he could master the Gauntlet, he would be ready to face Tree Top Gap.

Nut E. fidgeted and nervously bit his nails.

"Don't worry Nut E. It's not as hard as it looks," Champion encouraged. "You have come a long way. You have lost weight, and you are a lot stronger now. I am confident that you can do this. So relax, take a deep breath, and follow me."

Without warning, Champion took off, racing through the Gauntlet. Not wanting to be left behind, Nut E. quickly followed.

"Come on, C.J., let's go watch," Sammy said.

Sammy and I raced after Champion and Nut E. It amazed us how fast Champion could move. He spun, leapt, and dove from one branch to another so quickly it was impossible for Nut E. to keep up with him. But Nut E. refused to give up; he ran as hard as he could. Up, down, left, and right, he did everything he could to catch Champion. Still, no matter how hard he tried, he was just too slow. As I watched him struggle to drag his body atop a limb, and clumsily leap to another branch, I realized that he was not nearly as close to crossing the Gap as we thought.

Champion noticed Nut E. getting tired, and slowed down. "Come on, Nut E., you can do it," he yelled. Champion then ducked under a low hanging branch. "Watch out, Nut E. There   is . . ."

Champion tried to warn Nut E., but it was too late. Nut E. ran head first into the limb, and stumbled backwards towards Sammy and I. We grabbed him just before he fell to the ground far below. When Champion came over to us, Nut E. was out of breath and rubbing his head.

"I have done all that work," Nut E. said. "But nothing has really changed. I'm tired. My body aches. I'm still slow. And I'm too clumsy to even finish this Gauntlet thing."

Champion sat down beside Nut E. "Don't worry Nut E.," he said. "These things take time."

As Champion said this, Sammy leaned over and whispered into my ear.

"C.J., we don't have time. At some point, we're going to have to tell them that we can't stay any longer."

I felt frustrated. I didn't want to let the Mayor down, but I knew Sammy was right. Butterflies can't fly in the snow. And if we waited too long, we would never make it down to Butterfly Island.

We were still wondering if we should leave when we arrived at the river the next morning. Nut E. sat staring at his reflection in the water.

"How am I supposed to get across Tree Top Gap if I can't even run some stupid obstacle course?" Nut E. said, disgusted with himself.

At that moment, another reflection appeared in the water next to Nut E.'s. It was Butch. He was smiling from ear to ear as he walked up and patted the Mayor on the back.

"What are you looking for, Nut Eater? Another paint can? Well, that is not going to help you this time," Butch said sarcastically.

Nut E. gritted his teeth. "What are you doing here, Butch?"

"Well, I just came by to tell you that I have decided to run against you in the next election. The townspeople have all agreed that they are not going to vote for a squirrel that can't get across the river. So, if I were you, I would start looking for a new job."

Butch let out an evil laugh as he walked off into the distance. Nut E. looked scared, as he continued to stare into the water. I felt bad for him. I was going to say something to try and cheer him up, but before I could, I heard Rosie's voice.

"Okay, Nut E," she said. "It is weigh-in day. It's time to find out how much progress you have made this week."

Nut E. was still a little shaken as we made our way into Rosie's office. He slowly stepped onto the scale basket, and Rosie began loading the other side with stones.

"Seven . . . eight . . . nine . . . ten?" she said, as the basket lifted up off the ground.

"Ten!" Nut E. shouted. "Do you mean I have gained a stone?"

Nut E. jumped out of the basket and began yelling as the rocks in the other basket crashed to the ground.

"That's it! I quit! I have been working very hard, and now you're telling me I have gained weight?"

"Nut E., listen," Champion quickly said. "It is perfectly natural for you to gain weight. You are building muscle, which weighs more than fat does. Look at yourself," he said, pointing to Nut E.'s stomach. "Your stomach is smaller and your face is thinner. You look much healthier now. Just because that scale tells you that you weigh more, it doesn't mean you are not making progress."

Nut E. turned around and began walking towards the river. "Listen, everyone," the Mayor said. "I appreciate all of your help, but I am tired of being hungry. I'm tired of sweating. And I'm tired of feeling like a failure. I need to get across that river soon, because if I don't, I'm going to lose my job. I don't need some stupid Gauntlet to tell me when I'm ready. I'm ready right now."

"I don't think you *are* ready, Nut E.," Champion warned. "But it doesn't matter what I think. If this is your decision, then you should do it."

Rosie quickly hugged Nut E. "It's like my old uncle Finnigan used to say: 'If you push yourself too quickly, yourself might start pushing back.' Please, Nut E., if you're going to do this darn foolish thing, then at least try to be careful."

Everyone was a little worried about Nut E. trying to cross the river so soon, but Sammy and I were relieved. "This was going to work out perfectly," I whispered to Sammy. "If the Mayor can get across the river today, then we can leave for Butterfly Island this afternoon."

Word spread quickly. By the time Nut E. had climbed up to Tree Top Gap, a large crowd had formed below. Almost everyone was there, including Butch and his friends. Everyone, that is, except Champion. He had left right after the weigh-in, and hadn't been seen since. I couldn't believe he wasn't there to support Nut E. I know he didn't think Nut E. was ready, but the least he could have done was show up. As Nut E. looked out over the Gap, Sammy and I flew up next to him. He began shaking as he closed his eyes and took a deep breath. "C'mon, Nut E. You can do this," he whispered to himself, trying to build up courage. Just then, Kip came running up with Maggie. They stood beside Rosie on the ground and looked up at us. As I looked down at the huge crowd below, I thought to myself, *What if he doesn't make it? He will be humiliated.*

"Maybe you should wait Nut E. At least until you are more prepared," I said.

I couldn't believe what I was saying. All I wanted to do was to see Nut E. cross that river so that Sammy and I could leave for Butterfly Island. But over the past few weeks, Nut E. had become my friend. I didn't want to see him embarrass himself.

"Ahh, maybe you're right, C.J.," Nut E. said, looking down at Maggie. "Maybe I should do some more training first."

Nut E. headed back down the tree.

When Butch saw this, he began laughing and yelled, "Look, he's chickening out! I knew he wouldn't do it!"

Nut E. stopped. He stared down at Butch, gritting his teeth. His face turned angry. Then, glancing at Maggie, he turned and faced the other side of Tree Top Gap.

"Well, here goes nothing," he said, as he took a deep breath and ran towards the Gap.

He sprang off the end of the limb, and shot up into the air. At first, it looked as though he was going to make it. But soon his body began to fall. Nut E. panicked, waving his arms around wildly. The crowd cheered as he grabbed the branch on the other side of the river. But the cheers quickly turned to gasps as the branch bent and snapped. Nut E.'s body plummeted and splashed down into the middle of the river below.

Sammy and I flew down to him as fast as we could. When we reached him, Nut E. was swimming as hard as he could, still trying to get to the other side of the river. But no matter how hard he tried, it was useless. The current was just too strong. As the water swept Nut E. downstream, his face melted into sadness. Butch and his buddies laughed hysterically. A tear slowly rolled down Maggie's cheek as she ran along the side of the river. I, too, felt sad at that moment, for our chances of leaving anytime soon were drifting away down the river with Nut E.

The look on the Mayor's face said it all: he had completely given up. What little confidence Nut E. had gained over the past few weeks had shattered in just a few seconds. He obviously no longer cared what happened next. I began to worry until I looked up and saw something out of the corner of my eye. It was Champion. He was standing on the side of the river, holding a large stick out toward the Mayor. It was as if Champion had known what was going to happen, and had prepared for it. Nut E. grabbed the stick, and Champion pulled him to the shore. Nut E. just laid there on the grass. He was a rejected, defeated squirrel. It wasn't long before Butch and his buddies came out in the clearing where we were. Butch was carrying the broken branch in his hand.

"Look what you have done now, you big idiot. Now nobody can cross the river by using Tree Top Gap," Butch screamed.

Nut E. didn't even defend himself. He just sat staring out at the water.

"Now, thanks to you, the rest of us squirrels are going to have to pay turtle tolls like the small animals. You have ruined it for the rest of us, you incompetent fool!"

"Why don't you leave him alone," Champion said in an angry voice.

"How can you defend him?" Butch asked, holding out the branch. "Look what he did. He broke the branch. Now the Gap is too wide to jump. None of us can cross it now."

"I can still cross it," Champion said confidently. "And soon, Nut E. will be able to cross it too."

Butch laughed. "Are you kidding me? That tub of lard can't even cross the river by using Turtle Crossing, let alone Tree Top Gap, especially now that this branch is broke."

Champion glared at Butch. "Nut E. has been working very hard," he said. "He is losing weight, and he is getting into shape. He is going to cross that river, and he is going to do it soon."

Butch and his friends continued to laugh.

"It doesn't matter," Butch said. "Martin and Lewis have banned him from Turtle Crossing, anyway. They won't take him across, no matter how much weight he loses."

"He's not going to use Turtle Crossing," Champion said. "He's going to cross Tree Top Gap."

"This, I have to see," Butch sneered. "That beached whale will never be able to use Tree Top Gap now."

Champion had heard enough. He slowly walked over and looked Butch right in the eyes.

"Listen, tough guy," Champion began. "You know who I am, and I believe my record speaks for itself. So pay attention to what I'm about to tell you. The Mayor has a lot of friends who are helping him out, and together we will get him across that river. When that happens, I don't ever want to see you, or your friends, in Section 7 again."

Butch stopped laughing. "Wuh . . . wuh . . ." he stuttered, desperately trying not to look frightened. "Wuh . . . we . . . we'll just see about that."

As Champion chased Butch and his friends away, Sammy came over to me. I felt horrible as I stared at the shivering and humiliated Nut E. Squirrel. I didn't know what to do, but I knew we couldn't risk staying any longer. So when Sammy walked over and told me it was time to go, I had to agree with him. "I know you wanted to see Nut E. Squirrel get across the river," Sammy said. "But we have run out of time. Besides, Champion will see that he gets across."

I slowly nodded my head.

"Yeah, I guess you're right, Sammy," I said reluctantly. "Maybe we should go."

"Oh no, you guys can't leave now," Kip interrupted. "Champion can't do this on his own. You guys are the ones holding everything together. If you two leave, the Mayor will never get across the river. Butch will have him removed from office, and then he will take over. Do you really want your children to grow up in Mulberry Meadow with Butch as their mayor?"

"I understand what you are saying, Kip," Sammy said, frustrated. "But we have to leave before it starts snowing. And we have no idea when that's going to happen."

"I do," Kip replied.

"What do you mean?" I asked. "What are you talking about?"

"I know when it's going to snow," Kip said confidently.

Desperately wanting to believe him, I asked,
"So when is it going to snow?"

"When the cardinal comes," Kip said, smiling.

Kip explained that one of his bird friends, a cardinal from up North, always warned him a couple of hours in advance of the first snowfall. He told us that since the snow comes from the North, his friend had never been wrong. I couldn't believe what I was hearing. This was perfect.

"See, Sammy," I said. "Everything will work out fine. We will stay and help Nut E. until the cardinal comes, and then you and I are out of here. I promise."

Sammy agreed to wait for the cardinal, giving us more time to try and fulfill our promise to the Mayor. But Nut

E. looked as though he had already given up. I seriously doubted that he would be able to cross the river anytime soon. Nut E. needed help, and he needed it now.

I asked Maggie to try to speak to Nut E. again. I hoped she could get Nut E. to open up and tell her what was bothering him. Maybe that would give him the motivation he needed to complete the training and cross the river. Maggie agreed and slowly walked over and sat down beside Nut E. Neither of them spoke for a long time. Then, finally, Nut E., still staring out over the water, quietly said "Butch is right, you know. I broke the branch because I'm too fat."

Maggie didn't say anything. She just looked down at the ground. It was clear that she was very sad.

"I am so tired of being fat," Nut E. continued.

He was beginning to get very angry.

"It has haunted me my whole life. This world is very hard to live in, but it's even worse when you are a fat kid. Everyone treats you different. They make fun of you, and call you names. I remember when I was younger all the kids would laugh and make fat jokes. I laughed along with them, acting like it didn't bother me . . . but it did! I hated being fat then, and I hate it now!"

The more Nut E. talked, the angrier he became. "I was always picked last for sporting events in school.. Nobody wanted the fat kid on their team. I never got invited to any birthday parties because I never had any friends. Who wants to be friends with the fat kid? The only friends I had were adults, and sometimes I think they were just nice to me because they had to be. And girls? Huh, forget about it. No girl ever wanted to be with me. No girl wanted to be with the fat kid who sat on the bench during buckeye-ball games. The fat kid that finished last in every race he ran. I never went to even one school dance. I love to dance, but I could never get anyone to go with me. And why? Because, I'm fat!"

"I'm tired of being fat," Nut E. yelled. "And I'm tired of being alone! I'm a big fat squirrel, and no girl would ever want to love *me*!"

Maggie quickly turned and looked into Nut E.'s eyes. "That's not true," she said.

"Yes it is true, Maggie," Nut E. replied, looking away from her. "And you know it is."

"No, it's not," Maggie insisted. "And do you want to know how I know it's not true? Because I love you, Nuthaniel."

Nut E.'s mouth slowly dropped open as he looked back at Maggie.

"I have been in love with you for a long time," she continued. "I have just been too shy to tell you."

Nut E. began to smile.

"I really admire what you are doing, Nuthaniel" she said. "I know how hard it is for you, and I know how hard you have been working. You have not given up, and that is why I love you!"

Nut E.'s smile quickly faded into a look of sadness, and he turned back toward the river. "You don't want to be in love with me, Maggie," he said. "I might fail you like I failed everyone else who ever loved me."

Maggie seemed to understand what Nut E. meant. "Tell me about your brother Tommy," Maggie said in a sympathetic voice.

Nut E. appeared ready to protest. But his anger softened, and he quietly began in an ashamed tone. "I lied to you, Maggie. I *was* there when my brother drowned; and it was all my fault. It was a long time ago, but there is not a day that goes by that I don't think about it. We didn't have a father, and since I was the oldest, mom came to me when there were any problems. I will never forget that day when my mother came to me and told me that Tommy was lost in the woods. She was very upset and cried hysterically. Even though I was just a kid, I knew I had to say something to make her feel better, so I did. I told her that Tommy was going to be all right, and I promised her that I would not come home without him. I looked all day. I searched everywhere, but I couldn't find him. Then, finally, when it was almost dark outside, I decided to go look by the river." Nut E. paused before going on. "He was already in the water when I saw him. He had accidentally fallen in upstream, and was caught in the current. He was waving his little arms back and forth, and screaming for help." Nut E. paused again. "I ran after him as fast as I could, but I couldn't catch him . . . I will never forget the sound of his voice."

A tear ran down Nut E.'s cheek. "I tried to catch him, Maggie. I really did. But I couldn't."

Maggie put her arm around Nut E. and hugged him as he sobbed.

"I remember watching the water pull him under at Danger Rapids. I wanted to help him, but I couldn't. I couldn't get to him."

Maggie patted Nut E. on the back, held him tight, and whispered. "It's okay. It's okay."

"I let my brother drown, Maggie," Nut E. cried.

"It's not your fault, Nuthaniel" Maggie said, slowly rocking him in her arms. "It was a long time ago."

"You don't understand, Maggie," Nut E. replied. "I let my mother down. I told her Tommy would be all right, and he wasn't. He drowned. I promised her that I wouldn't go home without him, and I didn't"

Maggie looked at Nut E. confused. "What do you mean?" she asked.

"I never went home," Nut E. said, wiping the tears from his eyes. "I couldn't face her. I couldn't break my promise. I miss her, Maggie. I want to go home. She lives over there, and I can't get across this stupid river."

Nut E. got up on his hands and knees and began pounding his fists on the ground. "And why? Because I'm too fat! I just can't stop eating, Maggie. And it all started when I couldn't save Tommy."

Nut E. was now crying so hard he could no longer talk. Maggie began rubbing his back.

"It's not your fault Nuthaniel," she said. "You were just a child. There was nothing you or anyone else could have done to save your brother. It was the will of Mother

Nature. It was just Tommy's time to go. It's not your fault, Nuthaniel. You've got to forgive yourself. You are a kind-hearted beautiful squirrel. I know that you would never do anything to purposely hurt anyone. That is why I love you. I know in my heart that you can cross this river. And when you do, you will see that your mom doesn't blame you either. I'm sure she has never stopped loving you."

Maggie finished speaking. And though Nut E. continued to cry, I think he started to feel better. Maggie's words made a lot of sense. And for the first time in his life, Nut E. was beginning to let go of his guilt.

"You're right, Maggie," Nut E. said, nodding. "I feel a lot better getting all of that off my chest. Do you really think I can do this?"

"I know you can," she said confidently.

At that point, Nut E. gritted his teeth, and slowly crawled over to the edge of the river. He stared down at his reflection in the water and began talking to himself. "I can do this," he said clenching his teeth even harder. "I can do this. I will do this! I will be healthy! I will see my mother again!"

As Nut E. said this, a single tear slowly rolled off his face and splashed down into the water below. When it hit, it made the water ripple out in small circles which got bigger and bigger.

Nut E. told me later that as he stared at his reflection, the ripples of the water slowly took the image of the fat off of his body, and he was left staring at a thinner, healthier reflection of himself. For the first time in his life, Nut E. Squirrel was able to imagine what he would look like if he were healthy.

A huge smile covered Nut E.'s face as he looked over and took Maggie into his arms.

"Thank you, Maggie," he said. "I am done being fat and out of shape. I can do this. I know I can do this. I promise you Maggie," he said as he leaned down to kiss her. "Nothing short of the sky falling will keep me from crossing that river now."

Just then, a frantic voice screamed from above. "In coming!"

Looking up, I saw Peety the Chipmunk falling from the sky. He had two huge wings made of bird feathers tied to his arms. Apparently, he'd jumped from the tree overhead, and he was now falling towards the ground at a high rate of speed. He tried to flap his new makeshift wings, but they were useless.

"LOOOOOK OOOOOOOUT!" he yelled as he smashed into the ground.

His feet hit first, flipping him head over heels three times before he finally came to a stop. He lay there flat on his back, clenching his leg.

"Ah, my leg," he groaned. "Chipmunk down, chipmunk down . . . medic . . . medic."

Within minutes, Rosie O' Rabbit came running out of the woods, and began bandaging Peety's leg. Then two other rabbits loaded him onto a stretcher.

"You know, that test went a lot better than I thought it would," Peety said as he was carried away. "It was a huge success. I will be flying before you know it. This is where everything turns around for me. From here on out, I will be respected by every animal up and down the entire river."

At that moment, Peety became so excited that he fell off the stretcher and landed face first in the mud. We all laughed at Peety, but he was right about one thing: everything was about to turn around.

Closing the Gap

The next morning when we met everyone at the river, we saw a changed Nut. E. Squirrel. Having looked into his own reflection and picturing himself healthy, the Mayor wore the most determined look I'd ever seen. I knew that Nut E.'s body would now change because he had already changed his mind.

His eating habits were beginning to change as well. At breakfast, he surprised everyone by loading his plate up with mostly fruits and vegetables. Rosie could hardly contain her joy as she watched Nut E. munching away on a large orange carrot. Nut E. began to listen seriously to *everything* Rosie said. He sat for hours as she taught him the finer points of fruits, vegetables, and grains. Instead

145

of asking how something tasted, he now asked how healthy it was for his body. He ate much slower than he had ever done before, and he was beginning to truly enjoy the taste of each and every piece of food he put in his mouth. Because of this, his hunger was less, so he was eating smaller portions and he was actually leaving food on his plate. Also, he had stopped drinking saparilla. It was strictly water for this new and improved Nut E. squirrel. It was just as Rosie had predicted. Nut E. was beginning to fall in love with healthy eating, and his body was beginning to change.

Nut E.'s attitude towards exercise had changed as well. Determined to turn his life around, when it came to exercising, he was no longer willing to take no for an answer. Nut E.'s face looked focused and very serious. During stretching exercises, he let go of his fear and began to trust his body. For the first time, he reached down and touched his toes. He was very excited. He was doing better in the preparation phase of exercise, but as it turned out, he was just warming up.

As the day went on, Nut E. began to show a side of himself no one had ever seen before. He had run out of excuses, and was now making the most out of each and every exercise. As he moved on to resistance training, the Mayor shocked everyone with how many push-ups he could do. And when he began to struggle, he didn't quit. He just kept trying until the very end. When he moved on to pull-ups, he went right to work. The muscle in his arms began to bulge out from underneath his fur as he slowly pulled his body up into the air. When we all thought it was about time for him to rest, Nut E. just smiled and said, "I've been resting my whole life," and went right on working out.

I felt proud and excited. Not only had we helped Nut E. find the confidence to change his life, but because things were moving so smoothly I was sure that Sammy and I would have no trouble leaving before the cardinal came. This made me very happy, because I couldn't wait to see my wife Cat again.

Swimming came next, and like before with the other exercises, Nut E. was ready. He simply put his head down and swam as hard as he could. When Nut E. finally pulled his tired body out of the water, he had been swimming twice as long as he had ever done before. He looked tired, but wore a look of satisfaction on his face like he had finally broken through the bars of a cage that had held him prisoner for a very long time. As I watched the weary warrior make his way home that night, I found it hard to believe that this was the same squirrel who just a few short weeks before had fought against the idea of exercise, just because he was too afraid to try. But the Mayor's attitude toward exercise wasn't the only change; Nut E. was *thinking* differently and making better choices.

One day, as Kip and Nut E. stood talking by the river, I heard Nut E. say he was going to have a snack. I remembered the sap-covered nuts the Mayor liked, and how Sammy had raced to replace the gooey snack with a berry. Not wanting to be outdone by Sammy, I started flying towards Nut E. as fast as I could. Just as I was about to reach out and grab the snack from his hand, I saw something directly up in front of me. It was Sammy, and he was flying just as fast as I was. We crashed into each other right in front of the Mayor, and we both fell to the ground. As we sat there rubbing our aching heads, we looked up to find Nut E. smiling at us, proudly chewing on a carrot. We all just laughed as Nut E. continued eating his healthy snack.

It was so exciting watching Nut E.'s progress that I almost forgot about the oncoming snow. But Sammy and I took turns watching for the cardinal every day, knowing the time to leave would arrive soon. As we kept watch, the weather was getting worse, and each day was colder than the last. I knew the importance of our leaving on time, but Nut E. was getting so close to reaching his goal that I couldn't bring myself to leave before he had accomplished it. So I just ignored the weather, kept my eye out for the cardinal, and did everything I could to help Nut E. along.

Little by little, as Nut E. kept training, his body began to look and act differently. As his muscles grew, he became stronger. He could do more push-ups than before, and pull-ups became a breeze. And as his muscles grew, they began eating away years of fat. Nut E.'s round belly was disappearing, and his face got thinner. Every once in awhile, I would catch Maggie staring at him, and Rosie stopped calling him Nut E., and started calling him 'handsome.'

Champion was also happy with Nut E.'s progress. Their daily games of Tail Toss became exciting to watch. Nut E.'s body was so in shape that he was actually starting to give Champion a run for his money. Nut E. was making diving catches and his throws were now so fast and hard even Champion had trouble catching them. The two squirrels were becoming best friends. They spent so much time together that Nut E. began acting a lot like Champion. And as his body began to change, Nut E. was even starting to look like Champion.

Nut E. enjoyed exercising so much that once, when it was raining, Champion told Nut E. he could have the day off. Nut E. just smirked, and insisted on training in the pouring rain.

The next day, we were all sitting around watching Nut E. jump rope. Maggie was laughing and talking to him as he easily leaped over the rope again and again. Suddenly, Nut E. smiled and swung the rope over Maggie's head, down around and under her feet. She jumped it, and the two began jumping rope together. As they stared into each other's eyes, it was obvious how in love they were with each other. Nut E. was trying to build up the courage to kiss her, but just before their lips met, he got nervous and lost control of the rope. It caught under Maggie's feet, and they fell to the ground, laughing.

Later that day, Champion announced that it was time for another game of Tail Toss. As the two squirrels began playing, I could tell right away that something was different. Their games of catch were usually pretty lighthearted and fun, but this game was much more serious. Each of the two squirrels were playing as hard as they could, and the nut was flying incredibly fast. Champion would catch the nut, and whip it back immediately. He was no longer taking it easy on Nut E.; today they were playing as equals. Nut E. made one amazing catch after another, and I realized Nut E. was up to the challenge. He was spinning around and firing the nut back to Champion as quick as it had come. Champion didn't let up; he continued playing harder and throwing the nut faster. Each time, Nut E. would catch it and return it. Nut E. showed no sign of tiring. His training had paid off. All the swimming and jump rope had made his heart powerful. The push-ups and pull-ups had made him very strong, and the stretching had made him flexible.

This was obvious when Champion threw him a low one, and Nut E. simply dove for it, caught it, and returned it back to Champion before he even hit the ground. When the nut returned to Champion, he caught it in his tail and held it. Nut E. quickly jumped back onto his feet.

"What's wrong?" the Mayor asked

"Nothing," Champion said, smiling as though he had decided something. "How do you feel, Nut E.?"

"I feel great," Nut E. said. "So, here, throw it back."

Champion held the nut firmly in his tail. "No," Champion said. "I mean, do you think you are ready?"

"Ready for what?" Nut E. asked nervously.

"The Gauntlet," Champion said.

"Do you mean now?" Nut E. said, swallowing hard.

"Right now!" Champion replied, his eyes sparkling with excitement.

I couldn't believe what I was hearing. If Nut E. could successfully run the gauntlet, then he would be ready to cross the river, and our mission would be accomplished. Sammy and I couldn't stop smiling as the two squirrels made their way towards the nearby obstacle course. They climbed up to the starting line and were about to begin, when Champion turned to Nut E.

"Are you ready?" he asked.

"I don't know, Champion," Nut E. said, uncertain about running the Gauntlet. "Maybe we should wait until tomorrow. I'm feeling kind of tired."

At that moment, I heard a familiar voice coming from a branch off to our left. "Did someone say they're tired?"

It was the voice of Telly Vision. He popped out from under one of the branches. "What you need, my friend, is a little pick me up." T.V. started dancing back and forth singing a little tune. "Try Saparilla. It's the delicious drink that will help put a little kick—"

Suddenly, Champion leaned over and kicked T.V. off of the limb.

"In your ddddaaaaaaaaaayyyyyyy . . ." TV sang as he fell from the tree.

Sammy laughed as we heard T.V. splash down into the river below. Sammy might have been laughing, but Champion was very serious.

"Nut E., I know you are tired, but so am I," Champion said, getting back to business. "All you have to do is catch up to me and you will pass the Gauntlet. It's when you're tired and worn out that you find out just how strong you really are."

Champion put his arm on Nut E.'s shoulder.

"You can do this, my friend. I know you can," Champion encouraged.

Nut E. smiled. "Well then, what are we waiting for?"

Without warning, Champion took off. Nut E. wasted no time following right after him. I raced off after the two squirrels. Sammy, who was still watching T.V. pull himself up out of the river, was caught completely off guard. This was one race Sammy was going to miss out on.

I flew as fast as I could, dodging in and out of tree branches. Finally, I caught up to Nut E. He was moving incredibly fast. Only now could I see just how much progress Nut E. had truly made. He was amazing. He raced after Champion, leaping from limb to limb. I had to be very careful flying just to stay up with those two incredible squirrels. Nut E. was running, jumping, twisting, and turning doing his best to keep up with Champion. Champion dove off a branch, grabbed onto a vine and swung out around the tree, landing back on another branch heading in the opposite direction. Nut E. didn't even hesitate; he dove off the limb, grabbed the vine, swung around the tree, and raced after Champion before I even knew what was happening.

Then, suddenly, Champion tested Nut E. again. He grabbed a branch, pulled it along with him, and let go. The branch flew back at Nut E., threatening to knock him

The branch flew back at Nut E., threatening to knock him off the limb just like last time. But Nut E. ducked underneath it, and the branch whipped right over his head. Nut E. didn't even break stride.

The two squirrels continued racing through the trees, until finally Nut E. began to catch up to Champion. The Mayor kept reaching out to grab Champion's tail, but each time Champion sped up, leaving Nut E. with a fistful of air. But Nut E. was right behind Champion. Everything Champion did, Nut E. did too. It was like watching some sort of beautifully graceful dance. The two squirrels moved up and down, over and sideways, climbing and falling, until at last, Champion came to a screeching halt. Nut E. swerved to keep from running into him. I pulled up hard, and hovered next to the two exhausted squirrels. That is when I realized where we were: Tree Top Gap. As we stared out at the gap, it looked a lot further across since Nut E. had broken off that limb.

"There it is, Nut E. That space is the only thing standing between you and your mother. Tomorrow, she is going to see her long lost son again," Champion said.

Nut E. just stood there, his excitement fading to sadness. "No, she won't," he said. "Her son drowned a long time ago."

Nut E. lowered his head, and began making his way down the tree.

"What's wrong with him?" Champion asked, confused.

As I told Champion all about the story of Nut E.'s

brother, Tommy, drowning at Danger Rapids, his mouth hung open. A single tear welled up in his eyes and rolled down his cheek. Champion and Nut E. had become very close over the last few weeks, and he seemed to share his friend's sadness. Champion just stood there in silence for a moment, then slowly turned around, and walked away.

As I made my way down the tree, Sammy finally caught up to me. "What happened?" Sammy asked.

He was disappointed he had missed the race.

"Nut E. did it," I said, excited. "Champion says Nut E. is going to cross the river tomorrow."

Sammy smiled. "You know what that means?" he said.

"Yes, it means tomorrow we will be on our way south to Butterfly Island."

We were both so happy that we decided to find Nut E. and congratulate him on the completion of his training. We found the Mayor down by the river, talking to Maggie. Their conversation looked pretty serious, so we hung back a little and didn't interrupt them.

"What's wrong Nuthaniel?" Maggie asked, concerned.

"Champion says I'm ready to cross the river," Nut E. replied, reluctantly. "But I'm not. I am not ready to face my mother yet."

My heart sank. I couldn't believe that after all of his training Nut E. was still afraid.

Maggie looked surprised as well. "Nuthaniel, I thought we already went through this. There was nothing you could have done. Your mother will understand that. I'm sure she has already forgiven you. She just wants to see you again."

"I want to see her too, Maggie. I really do, but I just don't know if I can do this."

"Nuthaniel E. Squirrel, you are absolutely amazing," Maggie said, fervently. "You have accomplished so much in the last few weeks that I could not be more proud of you. You can do anything you set your mind to, and I think that is why I love you so much. I know in my heart that you can cross that river tomorrow, and I believe that you will."

Nut E. shook his head, and walked over to the edge of the river. "I'm worried, Maggie" he said. "What if I let everybody down again?"

Maggie smiled as she walked over and put her arm around Nut E. "Nuthaniel, you've already done so many amazing things that you couldn't possibly let us down. You are the squirrel that saved the river."

Nut E. just lowered his head, and looked down at the sun reflecting off the water.

"I don't know about that," he said, hanging his head. "Maybe Butch was right. Maybe I am a failure. After all, there are still no fish eggs hatching."

"Nuthaniel, look at your reflection," Maggie insisted.

"I know. I know," Nut E. sighed. "I can see myself healthy. But that doesn't change any . . ."

"No, Nuthaniel, look deeper," Maggie interrupted.

Looking deeper into the water, Nut E. gasped.

"Oh, Wow!" he said, stunned. "I . . . I can't believe it."

Wanting to see what they were looking at, Sammy and I quickly flew in closer and looked into the water. Nut E.'s shadow blocked the sun from reflecting off the surface, and we could see right into the river. Hundreds of baby fish were hatching out of their eggs and beginning a new life

"See," Maggie said. "The baby fish are finally hatching again. You did save the river."

Nut E. face changed instantly. The doubt in his eyes gave way to a look of confidence as he watched the baby fish swim around within his reflection. He smiled proudly and looked at Maggie.

"You're right, Maggie," Nut E. said. "I can do this. Tomorrow, I am going to cross the river."

Maggie looked at Nut E. and smiled.

"I know you will," she said. "And when you do, I am going to be there waiting on the other side with a surprise for you."

The following day was very cold. The wind blew hard, but it didn't seem to upset the determined Nut E. Squirrel. Word had already spread that the Mayor was going to try the leap again. Butch arrived early, hoping to watch Nut E. fail once more, and secure more votes to become the new Mayor of Section 7. Butch and his friends made fun of Nut E. as he climbed up the tree. Most of Tree Ville was there, and everyone was amazed at how healthy Nut E. looked.

"He looks pretty good," someone yelled out.

Then, another voice came from the crowd. "Yeah, but

can he make the leap now that the limb is broken off?"

As Champion and Nut E. stood on top of Tree Top Gap, Butch walked up to the base of the tree. "I know you're gonna fail this time, Nut Eater. Even I can't cross it now that you have broken the limb. It can't be done."

Nut E. looked nervous as Butch said this.

"Ignore that idiot," Champion said. "I know in my heart that you can do this. We have trained hard together, and now we're going to make the leap together."

With that, Champion backed up, ran as hard as he could, and jumped. He flew through the air very quickly, and landed so softly on the other side that the limb barely even moved. Butch's jaw dropped open. He shut up and sat back down with his friends. Champion recovered quickly, and then turned back to look at Nut E.

"Come on Nut E., you can do it," he said confidently.

We all held our breath, as Nut E. Squirrel stood alone at the top of Tree Top Gap. Everyone he knew was watching him from down below. Some hoped to see him make it, and others hoped to see him fail. I could tell he was scared. He reminded me of myself at the top of Lightning Limb so long ago, scared to move forward, and unable to go back. He just stood there shaking. At first, I thought he might give up, but then he saw Maggie. She walked out onto the limb across the river and stood next to Champion.

"You can do it," she yelled.

Nut E.'s face turned hard at that moment. His eyes fixed on the limb across the way, and he stretched his arms high above his head. Then he backed up and ran. When he reached the edge, he stopped. The crowd gasped nervously. He made a few more practice attempts, but each time, he stopped at the end of the limb. Then he lowered his head, and stared across the river. It seemed as if part of him was already there.

This is it, I thought to myself.

Nut E. stood there in silence for just a moment. Then he took a deep breath and began running. Each step came faster than the last, pounding toward the Gap. By the time he reached the end of the limb, he was running as fast as he could. The muscles in his legs tightened as he pushed off of the limb and sprang up into the sky. Nut E. flew through the air as if he had wings. He tucked his tail behind him, and reached out with his arms. I held my breath as Nut E. drew closer to the other limb. His arms waved around wildly, trying desperately to latch onto something. Finally, his hands hit the limb. He grabbed onto it, and held on as tight as he could, but then something terrible happened.

The limb began to bend just like before. The crowd groaned as the limb bowed to the point of breaking. Champion tried to help, but he wasn't close enough to make it in time. It seemed hopeless. Then Nut E. got mad, deciding that he was not going to fail this time. He reached up and grabbed the limb with his feet, and yanked himself forward until his body landed on the sturdy part of the branch.

The crowd exploded into cheers. I felt more proud

then than I had ever felt in my life. He had finally made it! Nut E. Squirrel had crossed the river!

The Cardinal Comes

All of Nut E.'s hard work had paid off. As he and Maggie reached the ground, the crowd surrounded them. Everyone cheered and congratulated Nut E. But no one was more excited than little Weedeater, who rushed up and tugged on Nut E.'s leg.

"I knew you could do it, Mr. Mayor," Weedeater said, jumping up and down. "And that's why, when I grow up, I want to be just like you."

Nut E. smiled proudly, and shook the tiny hand of the little rabbit.

"I knew you could do it, too," Maggie said wrapping her arms around him."You finally beat the river." She leaned over and kissed Nut E.

His face turned bright red. "Maggie, everybody is watching us."

"I don't care who is watching," she said, as she reached over and kissed him again.

I could tell that they were very much in love, and that for the first time, they were finally able to truly share their feelings with each other. Then Maggie drew back a step.

"Nuthaniel," she said softly. "Do you remember when I told you that I had a surprise for you? Well, here it is."

Maggie pointed over towards the woods. The crowd parted, and a very old female squirrel hobbled towards Nut E. She used two stick canes to balance her feeble legs, which shook underneath her.

When Nut E. saw her, his eyes widened, and his mouth dropped open. The crowd hushed, sensing that something special was about to happen. Nut E. could not speak. The closer she came, the more Nut E.'s face turned from smiles to tears. When she reached Nut E.'s side, he fell to his knees and took her hand. The female squirrel hugged Nut E. tight.

"I am sorry, Mom," Nut E. whispered. "I am so sorry."

Nut E. cried even harder. Nut E.'s mom just kept hugging tighter, until they were both slowly rocking each other. Nut E. spoke again.

"I let you down. I broke my promise to you. I am so sorry."

Nut E.'s mother reached down, lifted his chin, and

looked at him face to face. She tenderly wiped the tears from Nut E.'s eyes.

"Nuthaniel," she said softly. "I love you very much, and I'm so happy to see you again. Please don't cry. You did nothing wrong."

"Yes I did, Mom," Nut E. argued. "I failed you. I never brought Tommy home."

Just then, a shadow loomed over Nut E. and his mother.

"Yes, you did," someone said.

I quickly spun around to see who had spoken. I couldn't believe my eyes. It was Champion Squirrel.

"You didn't break any promises," Champion said. "You have brought me home."

At that moment, Nut E.'s mother looked up at Champion, staring deeply into his eyes with a strange look on her face. Then she slowly smiled and said

"Tommy . . . is it really you?"

"Yes, Mom," Champion said. "It is me. I'm here now."

As Champion walked over and hugged his mother, Nut E. immediately stopped crying. He just stared up at the two of them with a look of wonder on his face. None of us could believe what we were seeing. Champion was actually Nut E.'s long lost brother.

"But I don't understand," Nut E. said, puzzled. "I saw you drown."

"Well, I almost did," Champion said. "But when I reached the bottom of Danger Rapids and rounded the curve, The Great Owl of Light circled overhead. He swooped down and saved me just before I went under for the last time. He wanted to take me home, but I was lost in an unfamiliar place. He didn't know where I lived, and because I was so young, neither did I. So he took me under his wing, and raised me as if I was his own."

At that moment, Nut E. was speechless. I could tell he wanted to say something to his brother, but he couldn't find the words. Instead, he just stood up and hugged his family.

"Thank you, Nuthaniel," his mother whispered. "Thank you for bringing my baby home."

As the three squirrels reunited, Champion explained to Nut E. that he didn't know that he was his brother until the night before. Champion had decided not to tell Nut E. that morning because he knew it would get in the way of the jump. While the squirrels shared years of lost memories, all the pain of the past drifted away, and the love of family was all that remained. Everything, now, seemed to make perfect sense: the closeness of Nut E. and Champion, the desire of Nut E. to get across the river, and the pain and embarrassment he must have felt because he hadn't gone home. All the questions seemed to have been answered, and everything appeared to be all right. Nut E. had accomplished his goal, and saved his job. He was much healthier now, and he assured us that he had no intentions of going back to his old, unhealthy habits.

Sammy and I wanted to stay around and celebrate with everyone, but a bitterly cold gust of wind reminded us that we had overstayed our welcome in Tree Ville. It was time for us to start heading south. We quickly said our goodbyes. And just as we were about to leave, Nut E. walked over to Sammy and I and shook our hands.

"I can't thank you guys enough," he said. "I could have never done it without you."

Although it was freezing cold outside, the Mayor's words made me feel warm inside. Nut E. was a great squirrel, and I was honored to have had the opportunity to help him in his time of need.

"No, thank you, Mr. Mayor," I said. "Thank you for giving Sammy and I the greatest adventure we have ever had."

Everything had worked out perfectly, and I was anxious to get going. Just as Sammy and I were about to head up into the sky, I looked over at him and smiled.

"You see, Sammy," I said. "I told you everything would work out fine. You were worried about nothing."

Just then, something terrible happened.

"Hold on a minute!" Butch yelled, as he angrily walked up towards the crowd. "This isn't over yet." Butch who was obviously very upset, pointed towards Nut E. and yelled

"This squirrel is a fraud. I have just finished talking to the beavers, and they are still building the dam."

When I heard these words, my heart pounded against my chest, and I could barely breathe. Sammy looked just as shocked as I was. "This can't be true," I muttered. The crowd began chattering back and forth as everyone tried to figure out what was going on.

"What are you talking about?" Nut E. yelled with anger in his voice.

"The beavers told me all about what you did," Butch scowled. "They said that when you broke the limb off of Tree Top Gap, you thought you would never be able to get across the river. So you told them to start building the dam again." Butch had an evil smile on his face as he turned to address the crowd. "The whole meadow is flooding, and it is all his fault. I'm the squirrel you need. I would never have let this happen. I say we get rid of Nut E., and I will take over Section 7 like I should have a long time ago."

We all stood there in silence. Suddenly, Jackhammer the beaver came walking into the clearing. "Well, the dam is about finished, Mr. Mayor" he said as he held out a bill. "What do you say we go ahead and settle up now?"

Everyone looked at Nut E. in disbelief. What Butch was saying *was* true. "How could he have done this?"

Nut E. looked shocked as Butch yelled

"I say we string him up by his toes. We should put him—"

At that point, Butch was interrupted when Jackhammer walked up and handed him the bill. Butch's eyes widened, and he quickly looked around at the crowd, which was now staring at him.

"Ah . . . what are you doing?" he asked loudly. "This is not mine. It's his."

Butch pointed at Nut E. as he desperately tried to shove the bill back into Jackhammer's hand. He then cupped his hand over his mouth, and whispered loudly to Jackhammer. "What are you doing, you fool? Give this to me later."

Everyone heard what Butch was trying to hide.

"But I don't understand," Jackhammer said, confused. "We stopped building the dam when Kip told us to. Then you, Mr. Mayor, came up after Nut E. broke the limb off of Tree Top Gap, and told us to keep building. Don't you remember? You were all nervous, and kept saying how you couldn't get across the river anymore."

Jackhammer threw his hands up in the air as he turned around and began walking away. "You mayors really need to make up your minds," Jackhammer said. "One says stop, the other says go. Politics . . . who needs it?"

When Jackhammer left, everyone's attention centered on Butch. We all glared angrily at him as he slowly began to back up towards the river. He held his hands up in front of his body, as if to hold back the angry mob that slowly walked towards him.

"Okay, okay . . . you got me. I did it. I'm guilty. But you know what? Who cares if the meadow is flooding?"

I began to shudder with anger. "How could you do this to us, Butch? Our eggs are over there, and you know it."

Butch just rolled his eyes and shrugged his shoulders. "Ahh, who cares?" Butch said. "So what if I drowned a few bugs. It's not like I'm hurting any *real* animals."

I could no longer control the rage welling up inside me. I started to fly at Butch as fast as I could, but Sammy grabbed onto my shoulders and held me back.

"Don't do it, C.J.," Sammy said. "He isn't worth it."

"What do you mean, Sammy?" I asked angrily. "He's destroying our eggs."

"I know, C.J., but anger won't solve anything. We need to focus on the problem at hand."

"You're right, Sammy" I said, calming down. "I'm better than he is."

Butch now stood on the edge of the riverbank with his back to the fast moving water.

"All right . . . why doesn't everyone just relax . . . I think we can discuss this like adults." Butch shrugged his shoulders. "Hey, it's like they say: Let he who is without sin cast the first stone."

At that moment, Butch was hit right between the eyes by a flying turnip. He flew backward and plunged into the icy cold river. The crowd cheered.

Rosie looked up at a nearby tree, and shook her head, smiling. "I knew you would make me proud someday, Danny. I just knew it!"

Butch flailed his arms and legs back and forth and bobbed up and down in the water. "Help me!" he screamed. "I can't swim!" The current quickly pulled him downriver.

Sammy and I flew after Butch. By the time we caught up to him, he had rounded a curve and was very far downriver. Suddenly, I looked up ahead, and saw the dam. It was huge! It spanned the entire width of the river. Mason the beaver was working very hard to put the final touches on the huge structure. So when Butch floated up to him, Mason never looked up. He just pushed Butch's body up against one of the logs, and began mudding him into the dam.

Butch opened his mouth to protest. But when he did, Mason slapped a large tail full of mud in his mouth and smoothed it over his face. Butch's buddies, who had been running beside the river, quickly ran over and pulled him out of the mud. Standing atop the dam, Butch was completely covered in sludge from head to toe.

"Sammy," I said urgently. "We have to go check on our eggs."

A look of panic crossed Sammy's face. Together, we flew straight up into the air, heading towards Mulberry Meadow. My heart pounded as we raced to our children. "Please let our eggs be all right," I whispered to myself.

When Sammy and I reached the Mulberry Bush, a sick feeling rose in the pit of my stomach. The entire floor of the meadow lay under water, and it was rising fast. I couldn't believe that I hadn't noticed that the beavers had started building again. We'd gotten so caught up in Nut E.'s training that we never took the time to make sure everything was okay. The water was very close to our eggs now.

As we landed on the Mulberry Bush, Sammy looked around the meadow. "C.J.," he said in a worried voice. "Water will be up here soon. By the looks of things, I would say we only have a couple of hours before it reaches our eggs. We need to tear down that dam, and we need to do it now!"

"This is bad, Sammy," I said as I looked around at all the water. "This is really bad."

"It's worse than bad," Sammy said, staring up into the sky.

At first, I wasn't sure what he meant. Then I looked up and saw what Sammy was looking at. It was the cardinal. He was flying toward Beaver Tree Dam, and the snow was right behind him. Sammy and I both knew that if we didn't leave right then, we would never make it to Butterfly Island. We had run out of time. I turned to Sammy, and saw something that I had never seen before in my life . . . Sammy was scared. He didn't say anything, but I could see it in his eyes.

"What are we going to do, Sammy?" I asked, desperately looking for an answer.

Sammy slowly shook his head. "I don't know, C.J. If we don't tear down the dam, then our children will drown. But if we don't leave now, we will never make it. I think we . . ."

Sammy trailed off, staring at the eggs.

Then suddenly he asked, "What's that?" and pointed toward the eggs.

I looked over and saw an old brown leaf, rolled up and tied with Traveling Thread. It was leaning up against our eggs. I remember thinking that it was strange, because it was not there the last time we were here. Sammy walked over and picked it up. I couldn't believe my eyes when

Sammy took off the Traveling Thread and unrolled the leaf. It was the map. The map of Ponder Rock that I had drawn for Sammy so long ago. A tear rolled down Sammy's cheek as he read the words at the bottom for the first time:

In honor of Samson J. Caterpillar, who left his mark on the world by teaching me how to face my fears and believe in myself. He is my best friend, and the bravest Adventurer I have ever known. Thank you, Sammy!

Your friend,
Horatio Jones Caterpillar

"I can't believe it," he said. "We did leave our mark."

Sammy smiled and turned the map over. To my surprise, something had been written on the back. "Where did that come from?" I said. "I didn't write that." It was a message to the eggs, and Sammy read the words out loud:

To my Fellow Caterpillars,

Soon you will be born, and you will be faced with many different adventures. Some of them will be good, and some of them will be bad. But just remember that whenever you are in trouble, whenever things look bleak and hopeless, you should try to act like those two legendary adventurers, Horatio Jones Caterpillar and

171

Sampson J. Caterpillar. Their courage has inspired me throughout my life. Whenever I found myself in a bad situation, I tried to think what they would have done. I strove to be like them, and you should too. So when things are at their worst, just try to remember the most important lesson of them all. An adventurer never gives up! Even if he has to lay down his life to save another. I'm leaving you this map in hopes that you will be able to follow in the footsteps of the great adventurers who have come before you. Besides, I won't be needing this where I'm going.

Your friend,
Harold R. Caterpillar

I realized that this note had been written by the chubby little caterpillar I'd seen at the top of Ponder Rock on my first day as a butterfly. I guess he and his friend Stevie had used the map to improve their lives, and now he was handing it down to our children to help them live better lives, as well.

"We're not going down to Butterfly Island, are we Sammy?" I asked, already knowing the answer.

Sammy shook his head. "C.J.," he said. "Our lives will have meant nothing if we allow our children to drown here today. We have to stay and tear down the dam."

"I know," I whispered. I leaned down to the egg sack that held my future son. "Well, I guess this means you will be the man of the family now. I'm sorry. I know I promised to take you Cloud Climbing with me, but I guess you're gonna have to learn it on your own. Make me proud, son. And do me a favor will you? When you finally meet your mother, tell her I love her. Be brave . . . Be an Adventurer!"

Sammy said goodbye to his child, and we flew up into the air. I felt really sad as we flew back towards Beaver Tree Dam. Not because I wasn't going to make it to Butterfly Island, but because I was really going to miss Cat. "I love you, Cat!" I yelled out into the air. "Goodbye."

The air grew extremely cold as we flew towards the dam. Thin sheets of ice collected on my wings. It took all my strength to keep flying. When Sammy and I finally reached the dam, we immediately began clawing at the mud between the logs. My fingers were numb from the cold, but I knew I had to keep digging. We continued clawing at the mud for what seemed like an eternity. No matter how hard we tried, we could not loosen any of the logs.

"We're not going to make it, Sammy." I said. "This dam is just too big."

"We have to make it, C.J.," Sammy replied. "We have to save our eggs!"

Just then, I heard voices over on the riverbank. Looking up, I got a wonderful surprise. Champion, Nut E., Kip, Maggie, and Rosie and nearly every other animal that lived in Tree Ville came walking out of the woods.

They carried homemade shovels, picks, buckets, and a dozen other tools.

"Do you guys need some help?" Nut E. yelled, as they walked out onto the dam and began shoveling the mud away.

We are going to make it, I thought to myself.

When I looked up and saw how hard everyone was working, I was glad that Sammy and I had such good friends. But most of the other animals in the meadow had fur to protect them; butterflies weren't meant to be in this kind of cold. I was so cold, my teeth chattered uncontrollably, and I could no longer move my fingers. All I wanted to do was find someplace warm, but that was no longer an option. I just gritted my teeth and plunged my frostbitten hands into the nearly frozen mud, continuing to dig with every ounce of strength I had left.

My wings were nearly frozen solid. And the cold wind made my eyes water so bad that I almost didn't notice the huge white snow flakes falling from the sky. It was now official. There was absolutely no way Sammy and I could make it to Butterfly Island. I looked over at Sammy and our eyes met for a moment. Then, he just gave me a nod, and continued digging.

We all worked as fast as we could, but the water kept rising.

"This is hopeless!" Kip finally shouted. "The dam is just too big. The meadow is going to flood, and there is nothing we can do about it."

"What are you talking about Kip?" Nut E. said, frowning. "We can't give up. When I was down and out, these butterflies never gave up on me. Now they need my help, and there is no way I'm going to quit. If we stop now, their eggs will drown, and I am not going to let that happen."

When I heard Nut E. say this, I felt a lump in my throat. I realized then that when you care enough to help others, that generosity always comes back to you in one way or another. And while I was glad that Nut E. wasn't going to quit, I didn't know how he could save our eggs. The dam was just too big, and the mud had frozen solid. At that moment, Nut E. Squirrel surprised us all. He gritted his teeth, and stomped over to the biggest log on the dam.

"STAND BACK!" he shouted. "This dam is not going to be here much longer."

Then he reached down, grabbed on to the log, and began lifting as hard as he could. At first it didn't budge, and we all thought he was wasting his time, but then the most amazing thing happened. We heard the sound of wood cracking, and the giant log began to move. Water rushed beneath the giant log, heading downriver.

The crowd stood there in silence.

Nut E.'s newly developed muscles began bulging out from beneath his fur, as he continued raising the mighty oak log up into the air. The dam could no longer hold back the pressure of the raging river. I felt the other logs shifting underneath my feet, and the crowd scattered, racing towards the safety of the shore. When we reached it, we turned around just in time to see the remaining logs shatter into a thousand pieces.

Beaver Tree Dam was gone, and Nut E. Squirrel had saved the river once again.

The crowd roared with excitement as the water level began to drop. I sighed with relief as Sammy just looked at me and smiled. The meadow was no longer flooding, and our eggs were safe. Our children were going to live.

Everyone hugged and patted each other on the back. Maggie ran over and hugged Nut E. As the two began to kiss, I thought about Cat. With that, my excitement faded as I realized that I would never see my wife again. Sammy, who was standing next to me, looked as sad as I felt.

When Nut E. Squirrel saw the look on my face, he quickly quieted the crowd. "Wait a minute," he said. "I just realized something. You guys aren't going to make it to Butterfly Island, are you?"

Sammy just slowly shook his head.

Maggie gasped. "Oh no," she exclaimed, as tears slowly welled up in her eyes. "We've got to do something."

Everybody looked around at each other, but nobody seemed to know what to do.

Finally, Kip broke the silence. "If only The Owl were here," he said. "He could fly you down to Butterfly Island. But he's not back yet."

Desperately searching for an answer, Maggie looked at Nut E. and said

"What are we going to do?"

THE CARDINAL COMES

Suddenly, a not-so-thunderous hoot echoed throughout the meadow. I looked up into the sky, and couldn't believe what I saw. It was Peety the Chipmunk, and he was flying. He had completed his flying machine, and it worked perfectly. His little legs peddled furiously as two giant mechanical wings flapped above him.

"All is well!" Peety shouted, as he slowly came in for a landing and set the feathered aircraft gently down beside us. "How do you like my flying machine," he said, pulling off his nutshell crash helmet. "I finally figured it out. It was a simple matter of lift versus drag. It's quite easy if you think about it. Once I realized what the problem was, it was a cinch. Wow, I'm exhausted. I need a vacation. Maybe I will go down to Butterfly Island. Hey, wait a minute, aren't you guys going down to Butterfly Island?" he asked, looking over at Sammy and me. "I got an idea; we can go together. Hop in the back, and I'll give you a ride."

As Peety pointed to the flying machine, I couldn't believe what I was hearing. My mouth dropped open, and I felt wonderful. I looked over at Sammy, and he was smiling from ear to ear. We quickly said our goodbyes, and climbed into a large storage compartment just behind Peety's seat. The compartment had been filled with several leaf blankets, and Sammy and I quickly buried ourselves down into them to keep warm. Within minutes, I could feel the ice melting off of my wings. We held on tight as Peety flew us up into the air. Before long we were soaring high above the meadow. The warmth from the blankets felt great, and it wasn't long at all before the feeling began returning to my fingers.

"We are going to live," I said, as we started our long journey south.

Still smiling, Sammy reached under his wing and pulled out the flowers that he had bought from Telly Vision a few weeks before. He handed me one, and we toasted each other. The nectar tasted great as we sipped from the flowers. I leaned back and closed my eyes, enjoying the moment and the warmth that surrounded my entire body.

I was nearly asleep when I heard Peety yell, "Hang on fellas! Next stop . . . Butterfly Island!"